Chosen
A Child of Assault

A. M. LINTON

Chosen
A Child of Assault

A. M. LINTON

Hatred stris up strife, But love covers all
sins. — Proverbs 10:12
New King James Version (NKJV)

Dedicated to my loving, kind, strong and industrious mom.

God's blessings, always.

CHAPTER 1
A NEW JOB

Darkness slowly overtook January Island, and crickets chirped their songs of love and warning as nineteen-year-old James made his way home from work.

He pushed his hand into the front right pocket of his long black jeans and pulled out a keychain. The keychain was a silver booth with two silver keys hanging from it. He unlocked the cream-painted door and pushed it open, and even before one of his feet touched the white square tiles in the house, he called out, "Mom, Mom, where are you?"

"I'm right here," a melodious voice replied behind the door.

He pushed his head behind the door and saw her standing in the kitchen.

"Oh, hi," he said, smiling sheepishly.

"Hi," she sang out.

He closed and locked the door before bracing against it to untie and pull off his black and white athletic shoes. His white socks immediately follow. Next, he pulled out his dark blue T-shirt with the words "We Know Bikes" printed on the back of it from his black jeans and headed for the kitchen.

His mom, Janice, stood at the double stainless steel kitchen sink with a big blue teacup and a sod-filled rectangular sponge in her hands. Janice's black, curly, and shoulder-length hair was in cornrow. She didn't know how to plait her hair in cornrows, but she liked cornrows. So, ever so often, she would go to a popular salon to get it done. She had been there only a week ago, but presently, her hair was so well-kept it looked as though she had just been there a few hours ago. The back of her hair was in a bun, while the front was curled and placed on the right side of her head. Her naturally long eyelashes and thin eyebrows magnified her small brown eyes, and dimples, like sinkholes, appeared and swallowed pieces of her cheeks whenever she smiled. Dressed in a knee-length, short-sleeve, brown and white floral dress, it moved in harmony with her as she moved in front of the two kitchen sinks.

"Guess what? Oh no, don't guess," James said, smiling uncontrollably.

As he entered the kitchen, he exclaimed as his piercing brown eyes twinkled excitedly, "I've got it! I've got the job, Mom!"

"I knew you would. I told you so," Janice said, smiling up at him as she wiped her hands on a yellow dish towel on her left shoulder.

He nodded several times.

"Come here," she said, opening her arms.

James, smiling broadly, walked into her arms, and for a few seconds, she hugged him tightly.

He stood about three inches over her at five feet, seven inches. He shared his mother's light brown complexion, and on many occasions, he was told, "You are the spitting image of your mother." He did not have her dimples, though.

His curly high-top hairstyle, though neatly combed, needed a barber's touch.

"Congratulations, son! We must celebrate. How about us ordering a pizza or two?" she asked, holding him at arm's length.

"Pizza, yeah, sure, but in here smells so good. It smells as though you've already prepared supper."

He loudly inhaled while looking at the two stainless steel pots and cast-iron pan sitting on the grey grates of the cream and white thirty-inch stove facing him.

"I have," she said, looking up at him, "but it can keep until tomorrow."

"Mom, come on, you know me. I'll always choose your food over take-out," he replied, smiling and revealing white teeth with a small space between the two front ones.

Janice smiled broadly, and her high cheekbones rose higher, and her eyes glittered like light on dark water.

"Okay, okay," she said, "you go and wash up, and I'll set the food on the table. Then, you can tell me all about your new job."

"Okay," he said, turning and humming as he partly retraced his steps before turning to his right and walking down the short hallway to the washroom.

Dinner was on the table by the time James returned from the washroom. The dining room was next to the kitchen, and a waist-high, cream-painted wall separated them. He and Janice sat at the five-piece, brown-stained, circular dining room table. Steam from their plates of peas, rice, and curried lamb competed, and a glass of orange drink and cold water stood next to their dishes.

"O Lord," James prayed, "thank you for the new job and this delicious meal my mom has prepared. Please bless it to our bodies and use it for your glory. In Jesus' name, we pray, amen."

"Amen," his mom echoed and opened her eyes. She picked up the fork already on her plate and began eating.

They were lost in their food for several minutes as metal forks and porcelain plates entertained them with musical sounds.

"This is delicious, Mom," James said, laying his fork in his half-eaten plate of food.

He picked up his glass and drank half of its content.

"Thanks, son," she replied, looking over at him and shaking her head.

"What?" he asked, drawing out the word.

"I don't know how you can handle eating curry and drinking soda together."

"It's an art, Mom. It's an art."

"Yeah, yeah, I know. You've told me that many times before," she replied, smiling while picking up her glass of water.

For a few seconds, she stared at the floating ice cubes in the glass of water before putting the glass to her lips and drinking all of it.

"Which one of the jobs did you get?" she asked, putting down the glass, "If I remember correctly, you'd sent out about five applications?"

"Yes, and I got the one as a copy typist at Glen's Magazine," he said, a smile engulfing his face.

She matched his smile.

"That's great news, son."

"You know, Mom, even though I'd send out the other four applications, I was praying that this company would hire me."

He put a forkful of food into his mouth.

"Well, there you go. You've got what you've asked God for."

James nodded.

"Do you remember me telling you that about a month ago, the company got sold, and I didn't know who bought it?"

"Yes, I remember." She lifted the glass to her lips.

Some ice cubes had melted, and she allowed one piece of ice to enter her mouth. She crushed on it for a few seconds.

"Well, I now know who bought it."

"Who bought it?" she asked, putting down the glass and picking up the fork.

"The Wards purchased it, and as you might know, their son, Matthew, is living in Canada right now, but he will be returning here to help run the company."

The fork in his mother's hand slipped from her grip and landed on the porcelain plate before it bounced off and landed on the table. James saw it falling, but its sound after landing still made him jump. The noise clashed in their quiet home. He stared at his mom and saw that she was shivering, and the blood on her light brown face was all but gone. She was as pale as a whiteboard.

"Mom, Mom, are you okay?" He reached out and held her trembling hand on the table.

"I'm... I'm..." she said.

"Mom...," he called, jumping out of his seat.

His chair screeched across the tiles, but he didn't flinch.

"I'm... I need to lie down," she said quietly, looking up at him.

She gripped the chair arms and raised herself out of the chair, but her hands were still shaking, and she fell back into the chair.

"Here, let me help you."

He pulled back the chair and, taking her by the arm, helped her out of it.
James then led her down the short, narrow hall to her bedroom.

The cream-painted bedroom door was slightly ajar, and Janice pushed it open. Then, turning to him, she grabbed him by the shoulders and pulled him closer to her. Then she hugged him tightly.

"I love you, son," she whispered, then letting go of him, she turned and entered the room.

She closed the door behind her, and the lock clicked when it slipped into place. James turned and retraced his steps to the dining room. Frown lines creased his forehead.

Mom locked her door, he thought. *She never bolts her door.*

Behind the locked door, Janice crawled under the yellow and white sheet that covered her queen-size bed. The moment her head touched the sponge-filled pillow, her eyelids suddenly felt like boulders, and she struggled under the weight. After she pulled the sheet up to her chin, her lifeless hands collapsed on the bed, and she drifted into a frightful sleep.

CHAPTER 2
MISSING KEY

In 1979, on January Island, in the Parish of Bridgeport, on Greenville Street, sixteen-year-old Janice was lying on her double-sized bed.

She listened and sang along to Dionne Warwick on her new Sony Walkman. About two months before, she was given the Walkman by some visiting missionaries for memorizing the most Bible verses during their two-week camp in her village. The tape she was listening to belonged to her mother, but she enjoyed some of her mother's music. Gossip was floating around about Michael Jackson planning to release his first solo album, and if this were true, she could hardly wait to get her hands on it.

Janice's hair was plait in a cornrow bun at the middle of her head, and at the front, curls dropped on her forehead. Her mother did it several days ago. Janice's oval face and high cheekbones went well with the hairstyle. Well, at least, that was what her friends told her. As part of her nightly routine, she would put two curlers in the front of her hair to keep the curls. She then tied her head with a head tie to keep her hair neat for at least three weeks.

As she lay in bed, Janice had already done the nightly curling and tying her head to keep it fresh as long as possible. The bedroom door was slightly ajar, and light from the kitchen's fluorescent tubes kept the room from total darkness.

Janice was home alone, and one of her mother's rules was, "Keep your bedroom door locked at bedtime." Therefore, since that frightful morning, she started to obey that rule. However, tonight, the smell of rotting wood, due to the house's disrepair and the continuous rainfall throughout the day, made it too overwhelming for her to take. How could her mother expect her to close the door under these conditions when she was still awake?

Janice knew that it was for her protection that her mother had this rule, but she thought the house was too shabby for any thief to give it a second glance, and besides, they had nothing that a thief would want. So, in the past, she ignored the rule whenever her mother was at work. She would fall asleep with the door wide open, and in the early morning hours, when her mother returned home from work, she closed it. However, her mother would quarrel with her the following morning.

Then, one frightful morning about three months ago, she headed for the washroom after waking up, still tired and sleepy. She turned the doorknob, but the door didn't open. Her sleepy eyes automatically travelled down to the keyhole, and her hand reached for the long, silver, skeleton key, but it was not there. She looked down at the ground, thinking it must have fallen out of the keyhole, but it was not there either. She shuffled over to her dresser but couldn't find it there. She searched her hazy memories as though looking for a needle in a carpet. She then returned with what she already knew. She knew she had left the door open, and the key was in the keyhole when she drifted off to sleep. Then, her heart sank as a thought occurred to her.

"Mom," she whispered involuntarily.

Janice thought: *Mom took the key and locked the door from the other side.*

Janice walked over to her bed and sat on it for a few minutes before returning to the bedroom door. She was completely awake now and called out to her mother, but no reply came. She waited for a few seconds and then called out again. Still, nothing from her mom. She was on the verge of calling out again when a voice, rich and deep with sleep and muffled from behind two closed doors, said, "Maybe now you'll lock your door."

"I'm sorry," Janice replied, "I wouldn't do it again."

She paused, then pinned her ear to the door, listening for her mother's movements, but nothing came.

"Today's the class field trip. We're going to the airport and seeing the inside of an Air Canada aeroplane. I've been looking forward to this trip for a long time."
She paused, then listened, but nothing came.

"Please, Mom," she pleaded, her eyes swelled with tears.

"If you don't stop disturbing me, you'll be in there the whole day," her mother growled in a low, loud voice.

Janice jumped away from the door, and turning back to her bed, she threw herself into it and allowed the tears to flow like water through a broken dam. It ran down her cheeks and onto her pillow.

I'm going to miss the trip. Why does life have to be so hard?

Janice cried herself to sleep.

Sometime later, she was slowly drawn away from a frightful dream by someone shaking her arm and calling her name. Janice slowly opened her eyes, and her mother stared down at her with her light brown, circular, expressionless face. A black and white head tie covered her head, and she wore her favourite purple, white and floral sleeping dress.

"You still have about forty-five minutes to get to school before the bus leaves on the trip," she said, "You did say that the bus will leave at eleven, right?"

"Yes," Janice replied, nodding and rubbing the sleep out of her eyes.

"Lock your door," she said sternly, staring down at her.

Janice nodded vigorously.

"Hmm," her mother thundered before turning and leaving the bedroom.

Janice made it to school in time for the field trip, and although she still didn't share her mother's concern about thieves burglarizing their home, she began locking the door at bedtime. She dreaded a repeat of being locked inside her bedroom.

Nevertheless, with the door ajar tonight, Janice lay in bed wearing a knee-length pink and white polyester sleeping dress. She didn't know the words playing on the Walkman, so she decided to hum along. Janice knew that there was the possibility of her falling asleep while listening to the tape. However, she wasn't worried about it because she wasn't sleepy, and besides, she'd brought a glass of red Kool-Aid drink into the room, and the glass was still half full. She would drink all of it before returning it to the kitchen. Her mother didn't allow dishes in the bedrooms.

"They breathe cockroaches and rats," her mother told her.

"But most of the time, I only bring water in here," Janice protested sometimes.

"It doesn't matter; an empty glass is still a dish, and that's all those cockroaches and rats care about," was her mother's usual response.

"Okay, Mom, okay," Janice would say, and that was the end until her mother found another glass in her room.

However, since the door incident, Janice didn't know what her mother would do if she found more dishes in her bedroom. So, she wasn't going to take any more chances. She wasn't going to put her to the test anymore.

CHAPTER 3
THE STRANGER

Janice's double-size bed was at the far left-hand corner of the room, next to the only window in the bedroom.

A cherry-red curtain whose bottom rested on the aged, brown vinyl floor covered the wooden louvres. A three-piece dresser stood opposite the bed with some white paint peeling off. Also, she neatly stacked a short blue and white deodorant bottle, a long pink and white body spray, a black comb with a few missing teeth, and several books on top of the dresser. A purple and black backpack and a pair of black school shoes were at the dresser's feet. A blue and white, slightly over-the-knee school uniform was also hanging on the back of the bedroom door.

Janice closed her eyes and adjusted her hands behind her head as she listened to Dionne Warwick, who took her to unfamiliar places through her words. Suddenly, her heart skipped a beat, and all the hair on her body stood at attention, and she shivered as darkness filled her closed eyes. Like a spring, her eyes flew open, and she stared at the silhouette of someone standing in the doorway. Fear, like an anesthetic injection, paralyzed her. Her heart became a trapped steel drum in her chest.

The silhouette entered the room, and suddenly, a bright light from a torchlight blinded her. Suddenly, it disappeared, and the stranger quickly covered the distance between them, and he was on the bed, straddling her. He pushed the torchlight into his pocket before removing the headphones from around her head.

"Please... please," Janice pleaded, finding her voice. "Please don't hurt me. Take..., take whatever you want, and I won't stop you."

"I'm not going to hurt you, Janice. I'm only here to please you," the stranger said in a deep, slow, baritone voice.

"How... how do you know my name?" she stammered as the steel band in her chest grew louder.

"I've been watching you, Janice," he said.

"Please..." Janice said.

"Turn over," he said, interrupting her as he lifted his body off her.

She froze.

"Come on," he said, helping to turn her

stiffened body onto her stomach. With this done, he pinned her arms behind her back.

"I hope the music puts you in the mood. I heard you humming when I was at the door," the stranger said.

Scream, scream, her brain cried. So, she lifted her head from the pillow and screamed.

"Help! Help!" she cried, praying that someone would hear her cries.

"What... what are you doing? Stop that because someone might hear you," the stranger said, surprised.

He let go of her hands.

"What?!" Janice asked, coughing.

"You can scream, but not so loudly," he said, "it's still early, and besides, it's Friday, so a lot more people are still out and about."

What? This guy is crazy! Oh no, I'm going to die! He's a madman. Did he escape from the mental hospital?

She silently searched her memories for news of an escapee from the island's only mental hospital. Then, suddenly, she was brought back to the present by what felt like handcuffs pinching her skin.

She cried out in pain.

"Sorry, sorry," the man said, "let me take it off. We wouldn't need it. We can do this without it."

He was straddling her again.

"Please," Janice pleaded again, "if you

leave right now, I wouldn't tell anyone you were here."

He didn't reply but lifted his body a few inches off of her and pushed his hand into his pocket, and she heard a soft jingle, and within seconds, the handcuff was off.

Janice suddenly and violently jerked her body, trying to throw him off her back. He jumped off the bed and stumbled a little before he caught himself. His hands quickly moved to his back, and he drew something from behind it.

"That's it!" he whispered loudly, "I didn't want to go there, but you've forced me. Don't move a muscle, or I'll shoot you!"

Janice was rolling off the bed and about to carry out the rest of her plan of crashing into him before running through the door and locking herself in the washroom when he spoke. She froze, her feet touching the ground.

What? Does he have a gun? her frantic mind exclaimed as her eyes shifted to his hand, and indeed, she could make out what looked like a gun in his right hand.

"Now," he said, exhaling slowly and loudly, "we're finally getting somewhere."

The stranger slowly walked back to the bed.

"Lay on your back, now!" he commanded.

"Please…" Janice protested.

"Not a word," he said, shaking the gun from side to side.

Although trembling, Janice did what he said, and he climbed into the bed after her. Once more, he lightly sat on her, but a little lower than before. He took the gun and slowly moved it from her chest to slightly past her navel.

Janice shivered in fear.

The stranger stretched out his body on top of hers and moved rhythmically.

Oh God, please help me. Please help me, she silently pleaded.

He lowered his head and slowly licked, then kissed the sides of her neck. She shivered again, and her body grew even stiffer.

"You smell so nice," he whispered as his hand moved up and down her left arm.

"Please… please don't do this," she cried through trembling lips.

His hand stopped moving, and he grabbed her nightdress, trying to pull it up, but it protested.

"Don't worry," he whispered, as his breathing grew more profound, "I'm going to make it good for you. You'll see, I promise."

She wanted to scream again. She wanted someone to help her, but her throat suddenly felt as though it was full of sand.

"Don't go anywhere," he said, spit dribbling out of his mouth and landing on her neck.

Janice jumped when the wetness hit her neck, and for an insane moment, she thought he had shot her.

"Sorry," he said, wiping his mouth with the back of his hand, and got off the bed.

She heard his voice, but she didn't listen to what he said. Her eyes followed him in the darkness, but the rest of her body did not move, and she saw when he put the gun into his pants pocket before dropping his pants to his ankle and stepping out of it. She heard a quiet thump when the pants reached the floor, and she jumped again. He pushed his hand into his shirt pocket and pulled out something. Janice heard the soft rustling of plastic, and her heart mourned in anguish but relief at the same time, and a groan rattled in her throat.

Her groan was followed by a few seconds of silence.

Oh God, Janice pleaded, *please let me die.*

The stranger returned to the bed.

"Help me with your clothes," he said, tugging at her uncooperative nightdress, "Don't try to fight me. The sooner we're finished, the happier you'll be."

Janice, trembling, lifted her body about an inch off the bed, and this time, when he moved her clothing, it did not protest. He then raised the nightdress to her waist, and after removing her undergarment, he lowered his naked body on hers, and the invisible sandbags holding back her tears washed away. Time stopped for Janice, and pain radiated between her legs as the stranger violated her.

Time began again when the stranger rolled off of her. He laid on his back, breathing heavily.

"Wow! That was spectacular!" he exclaimed.

Janice was silent as her brain screamed for her to do something. Anything!

"Well," he said, propping on his elbow and looking at her face, "was it what you paid for?"

I'm dreaming; I'm having a nightmare. I'll pinch myself and wake up, Janice scattered mind thought as hope jumped into her heart.

She slowly moved her hand closer to her leg and pinched it hard. She felt the pain and bit her lower lip to keep from crying.

"You know when you suggested that I walk with a real gun and not a fake one, I didn't think it was a good idea, but boy, I was wrong," he continued, "It got me going."

"What are you talking about?" Janice asked in a quiet, trembling voice as tears streamed down her cheeks silently.

"You know, the job is over now, so you don't have to keep pretending," the stranger said.

Janice took in a trembling breath.

"Wait, are you crying? You sound like you're crying?" he asked, reaching out and passing long fingers across her cheek.

"Look, even though you know me, I don't know you, and I didn't ask you to do this to me. So I don't know what you're talking about."

As though scourged by fire, the stranger ripped his hand from her face and jerked away. He fell off the bed and scrambled for his pants on the floor. He stumbled as he struggled into his pants, and his hand flew out to the wall for help, and it landed on the light switch. The sudden brightness in the room stung her eyes, but it did not blind her because the tubal fluorescence lighting in her room needed replacing. It was dull. She stared at her attacker, and he froze for a few seconds before spinning around, turning off the light, grabbing at the door, flung it open and fleeing from the room.

Janice strained her ears to hear his retreating footsteps, but the drumming in her chest was too loud for her to hear anything else.

Matthew Ward, Matthew Ward, her

mind screamed, but she shook her head, commanding it to stop lying to her. *It was someone who looked like him. It could not be him.*

Still, her mind refused to be silent and cried out again.

Matthew Ward, Matthew Ward.

She shook her head again, and this time, it stopped screaming. Fresh tears filled her eyes, and as they threatened to become waterfalls, she clenched her teeth and said quietly, "No. No. I will not cry. I will not cry." Then commanded, "Get up, get up, get up," Her heartbeat continued to drum in her ears, and she sprang off the bed, grabbed the bedroom door, closed it, and locked it.

The room plunged into total darkness.

Janice tried to slow her breathing, and the big toe on her right foot began throbbing as she did. It felt as though she'd stumped it on something, but she didn't see how she could have done so. There was nothing on the floor between her bed and the door. Nevertheless, she lifted her left foot and pressed down on the toe for a few seconds. The pain slowly subsided, and her anger slowly rose as it did.

Her eyes adjusted to the darkness, and as she looked around the bedroom, she breathed deeply, hoping to calm her rising anger. Instead, it increased her anger. She suddenly dashed to the dresser and knocked everything off with one hand sweep. She felt for the drawers and yanked them out of their home before throwing them across the room. When the drawers were gone, she turned to the bed and grabbed the mattress. She flipped it into the air, and within seconds, it landed with a soft but determinate thud on the spring frame. The springs cried out, but Janice ignored them as she fumbled to regain a firm grip on the mattress again. Finally, she got hold of it and was about to throw it into the air when she heard the faint sound of jingling keys.

He's still here! Janice thought, and like a deer caught in the headlights of a speeding car, she froze. Her brain screamed, and the weight of the mattress caused her arms to lower involuntarily, and she quietly allowed it to rest crookedly on its frame.

She stood there frantically looking around the room for something to defend herself.

"Janice, Janice," an angry but familiar voice called, "how many times am I going to tell this girl not to open my bedroom window when I'm not here."

"Mom?" Janice whispered as her mind tried to process what was going on.

She heard the thud of the window when it was closed, and distant footsteps immediately followed this.

"Mom?" she whispered again but a little louder.

CHAPTER 4
A PHONE CALL

Sometime later, Janice sat in the living room in a red, well-worn, single-seat upholstered chair. She gazed unseeingly at the steam rising from her hot cocoa as her thoughts consumed her. Janice wondered about her mother's tenderness towards her as she carefully wrapped a yellow sheet around her shivering shoulders. Then, for a second, she questioned if an alien replaced her mother.

"Why me?" she asked. "Why did this happen to me?"

"I don't know, Janice, but asking that question will not get you anywhere. You have to put it behind you and move on," her mother replied as she walked over to the long sofa opposite where Janice sat.

"How can you say that? I... I was just... attacked," Janice said, and for the second time since her mother returned home, she unexpectedly burst into tears.

Yes, Janice thought, trying to control

her tears. *This person is not an alien. This person is indeed my mother.*

After hearing her mother's grumblings about her not locking the window and her angry call to her, Janice slowly reached out for the door with trembling hands. She slowly turned the brass knob, but nothing happened. Then, remembering locking the door, Janice slowly turned the key in the hole and quietly pulled it open. She tiptoed out of her room and was almost at her mother's bedroom door when her mother appeared. Her mother jumped in surprise, but that did not stop her hand from flying to her side to retrieve the dark brown wooden baton hanging there.

"It's me, Mom. It's me, Janice," she called out, flinging her hands to protect herself.

"Girl, what are you doing? Why are you sneaking around in here?" she exclaimed.

"Shh, shh," Janice whispered, with a finger to her lips, "someone broke in just now, and I think he's gone, but ...."

"Go back to your room and lock the door until I tell you it's okay to come out," she commanded, looking around her.

Janice hurried back to her room and locked the door. She pressed her ear to the door, listening for her mother's movements, but could hardly hear anything. Then, after what seemed like an eternity, her mother knocked on the door, saying it was safe for her to come out. At that, Janice switched on the bedroom light, turned the key, and pulled open the door. Her mother entered the room but stopped suddenly as her eyes travelled around her.

"He did this to your room?" she asked, astonished.

Patsy Shepherd was Janice's mom and was known as Ms. Shepherd in the neighbourhood. She was a tall, big-boned woman, and as she stood inside the room with the baton still in her hand, she looked a lot more intimidating than Janice had ever seen her. Her light brown skin, Jerry Curled hair, and rosy cheeks usually gave her face a tenderness that her deep brown eyes did not hold. However, as she stood there, her face matched the hardness that her eyes usually have.

Janice slowly surveyed the room. Clothes were scattered across the room, and drawers were on the floor. Two drawers were between the bed and the wall, and the mattress was crooked on the frame. She ripped her eyes away from the bed and glanced at her mother.

Why is she still in her uniform? Janice wondered.

Her mother wore blue pants and a light-blue, short-sleeved security uniform. *She never wears her uniform outside of work.*

"Janice?" her mother asked.

Janice cleared her throat, trying to find her voice.

"The guy. The guy who broke in, he … he attacked me," she said.

"Attack you. What do you mean by attacked you?" her mother asked, replacing the baton to her side.

"I was lying on my bed, and when I opened my eyes, he was standing in my bedroom."

As she ended her sentence, she took a few steps away from her mother.

"Wasn't your bedroom door locked?" she questioned sharply.

"I wasn't ready to sleep," Janice protested as tears stung her eyes.

Her mother glared at her, and Janice watched as anger distorted her face.

"Little girl, little girl," she boomed.

Janice stepped farther away from her.

"I've told you repeatedly to lock your bedroom door when I'm not home and not open my bedroom window, and still, you wouldn't hear me," she said, shaking her fists.

"I didn't open your window."

"And I didn't leave it open. I locked it before I left. I always do," her mother replied.

"This is not my fault," Janice said, as

tears ran down her shrunken cheeks, "I didn't even go into your bedroom when I came home today."

Her mother opened her mouth to speak but immediately closed it and dropped her hands to her sides. Her face softened a little.

"I'm not saying that—"

"I need to take a shower," Janice said, cutting her off as she rushed through the bedroom door.

"Wait," her mother called, "When you said that he attacked you, do you mean that he... he... forced himself on you? I mean, did he force you to have ..., intercourse?"

Janice stopped and slowly turned to face her mother, but she looked down at her feet.

She nodded. "Yes, once."

Her mother sighed before saying, "Then you can't take a shower. I have to call the police and report this."

"No!" Janice said, practically shouting the word, lifting her eyes to meet her mother's face.

"What?" her mother asked in astonishment.

Janice lowered her head, averting her eyes again. She did not want her mother to see the fear she was holding. She was afraid that it would reflect on her face. Her mother usually did an excellent job of reading her.

"It will take them hours to get here, Mom, assuming they'll even bother to come. Then, they'll somehow make me feel it's my fault. You know how they are, and besides, I can't stay like this for that long," Janice said. "I know a woman who works there. I'll talk with her, and she'll come quickly."

"I have to shower, Mom," Janice pleaded, trying to press down her rising fears, "I can't stay like this anymore."

"The police will believe you more if they get the evidence on you," she said.

"Believe me more? Mom, even if they bother to come by some miracle, they will blame me, no matter what evidence they get. I can't stay like this for hours."

Janice shivered before turning to enter the washroom that was opposite her bedroom.

"You are exaggerating, and besides, I've already told you, I know a policewoman stationed there; she'll come quickly," her mother said.

"But what if she's not there or can't come soon?" Janice asked, stopping just inside the bathroom.

"Then we'll have to go to the hospital."

"Hospital... hospital," Janice said, squealing like a mouse.

"Yes, we have to report this." Her mother walked closer to her.

"No, I'm not going to a hospital, and you can't make me go."

She backed away from her mother.

"Okay, okay, let's not get ahead of ourselves. Let me call the police station, and we'll take it from there."

Janice opened her mouth to protest.

"I'm making the call," her mother insisted.

She walked away from Janice and went into the living room. Janice could hear the pages in a book turn before her mother picked up the telephone receiver and dialled a number. Janice stood inside the bathroom and tried to listen to her mother's conversation. She couldn't hear her mother's words because she was speaking quietly. So, Janice began pacing in front of the washroom.

A few minutes later, her mother returned to tell her that the policewoman she knew was on vacation. The officer who answered the phone said he could send out two officers within three hours. However, her mother told him not to.

Janice slowly breathes a sigh of relief. She didn't realize she was holding her breath.

"I should still take you to the hospital," her mother said.

"I don't want to go, Mom," she said, "I need to shower."

Then, before her mother could say anything else, she backed into the washroom and closed the door.

"Okay, okay," her mother said, throwing her hands into the air, "Have it your way."

Janice locked the washroom door and braced against it, trying to stop her trembling. The bathroom was average size and painted in peach. A miniature painting of a girl kneeling in prayer was also above the sink.

Janice took a deep breath before swiftly ripping her pink and white sleeping clothes over her head. She threw it into the room's far corner and glared at it for a few minutes. Then, slowly, she walked forward, pulled the floral shower curtain and the plastic curtain behind it aside, and stepped into the shower enclosure. The small shower area was made entirely of concrete. The silver shower head was slowly rusting, and although gunk was on it, it was not enough to stop the water from flowing forcefully out of it. Absentmindedly, she turned on the shower, and cold water gushed out, hitting her lower body. She slowly stepped back, giving it a few minutes to warm up, before stepping forward again.

Then, after what seemed like a few minutes, in the shower, Janice heard her mother banging on the door.

"Janice, Janice," she called, "It's time to come out."

Janice looked down at the brown wash-cloth in her hand and wondered how it had gotten there. She didn't remember pulling it off of the shower rod. Janice let the cloth slip from her hand, landing with a wet *plop* on the concrete floor. The water temperature had moved from warm to hot, and steam surrounded her, but she took no notice of it. Her mother knocked and called out again.

"Okay, okay," she called out as she reached out to turn off the tap.

"Here," her mother called out from outside the bathroom, "I have some clean sleeping clothes for you to put on."

Janice stepped out of the shower and wrapped the orange and white towel hung behind the door around her. She unlocked the door and pushed it slightly open. She took the clothes, murmured, "Thank you," and locked the door before slowly dressing in them.

Now, as Janice sat in the pink, green and cream floral upholstery loveseat in the living room with her fingers looped around a cup of hot cocoa, tiredness suddenly overwhelmed her, and she yawned.

"Are you ready to tell me what happened here tonight?" her mother asked, moving forward to sit on the edge of her chair.

"What do you mean?" Janice asked, frowning.

She lifted her head to meet her mother's eyes. Her mother was sitting opposite her in the long chair.

Her mother was silent as she searched her face, seeking answers to the question she'd asked. Janice waited for her to answer her question.

"Do you know who it was? Were you able to see his face?" her mother asked after a few seconds.

"I don't know who it was, and I didn't see his face," Janice mumbled, lifting the cup to her lips as she lowered her eyes.

"Was it, Roger?"

"Roger?" Janice almost choked on the hot cocoa in her mouth. "Why would Roger do this to me? Roger would never do something like this to me."

"Then who was it?" she asked.

"Roger cheated on me, and that's why we broke up. He's not a..., he's not a..., he's not that kind of a guy." Janice added, "But then again, what do I know?"
The smell of the cocoa filled her nostrils, and she emptied the cup with one mouthful.

"Then who did it?" her mother asked, her voice rising slightly.

"I don't want to talk about it anymore. I'm too tired to think anymore."

"What's there to think about?" her mother asked. "Who was it that attacked you?"

"I don't know," Janice's voice raised slightly.

Her mother exhaled loudly. Then, slightly moving her body, she braced back in the chair.

"Why are you home so early?"

Her mother sighed, sat up, and shook her head. Janice looked down at her empty cup.

"There was a mix-up with the schedule at work," she finally answered, "This new supervisor doesn't know what he's doing."

"Oh, okay," Janice replied as another yawn escaped her. Then, after a moment of silence, she said, "I'm going to my room." However, she did not attempt to move.

"I'm taking you to the police station in the morning. You need to make a report."

"I'm going to my room."

She jumped out of the chair and draped the blanket around her. She walked to the kitchen, quietly placed the cup in the empty stainless-steel sink, and returned to the living room. She murmured goodnight to her mother and hurried off to her bedroom. The bedroom door was partially open. She reached for the doorknob and opened the door, but her feet refused to move. Move, she silently commanded them, but they did not obey.

"This is my room, my room," Janice hissed through clenched teeth.

Walk, walk, she commanded again, but they still refused to move.

She pushed the bedroom door and, leaning her upper body through it, stretched out her hand and felt along the wall for the light switch. She found it and turned it on, and her mouth fell open because of what she saw.

Her room was no longer in disarray. A light brown sheet and matching pillowcases had replaced the previous coverings. Also returned to their original places were the drawers, clothing and other personal items.

"Wow," she whispered, and to her surprise, she found herself standing inside the room. She closed and locked the door.

Janice braced at the door and looked around the room. She fought with her memories and slowly walked over to the bed. Janice picked up the pillow and the folded cover sheet sitting on it. She unfolded the sheet and tucked herself into a ball before covering herself with the sheet.

CHAPTER 5
SURPRISES

The following morning, Janice was slowly drawn away from a deep sleep by the crowing of roosters. Her neck was stiff, and her entire body ached. She cautiously pulled herself into a sitting position, and a frown slowly formed.

Why am I on the floor?

Her head throbbed, and like an unplugged sink, it ran the previous night's events to the forefront of her mind, and she struggled to stay afloat.

Oh God, she silently pleaded. *What am I going to do?*

The roosters crowed again, drawing her attention to the outside of the house. She could hear a vehicle being driven slowly down the potholed street. Janice wondered if the driver was returning home or on an early Saturday morning errand. She jumped when a familiar thump on the front door attracted her attention.

The newspaper is here, but I don't want

to go outside. Then, *get a grip of yourself, girl,* she thought. *It's not as though he's outside waiting for you.*

He's gone. The guy is gone.

With that, she struggled to her feet, and a few minutes later, her cheeks were flushed because of the slightly cold early morning breeze. She plumped down into the loveseat in the living room and sighed quietly. She unfolded the newspaper, shook it firmly but gently, and straightened it. She looked down at the front page, and a quick, sharp scream escaped her. The papers dropped from her hands, and she jumped out of the chair. The newspapers landed on the multicoloured floral rectangular mat on the polished floor.

She shivered.

"Jan!..." her mother called.

The creaking of the floor immediately followed this as her mother got out of bed and opened her bedroom door.

Janice, still shivering, struggled to slow her heartbeat. She stooped and quickly picked up the newspapers from the floor. She dropped into the chair and opened to the middle of the newspaper seconds before her mother entered the living room.

"What's the matter? Are you okay? I thought I heard you scream," she said, looking around the room.

"Oh," Janice said, pretending to be surprised by her mother's sudden appearance, "it was just something in this newspaper. I just don't know what this world is coming to."

Janice shook her head, pretending to be deeply affected by what she was reading.

"You got me out of my bed because of a news story?" her mother asked in vexation.

"I'm sorry," Janice mumbled, looking up at her briefly. "I didn't mean to wake you, sorry."

Her mother let out a lengthy stiups before turning and walking back to her bedroom, mumbling to herself. She slightly slammed the bedroom door behind her. Janice slowly released her breath and turned to the newspaper's front page.

She held her breath and stared at the photo of a smiling Matthew Ward with his parents, Oliver and Nancy Ward. The article praised them for their contribution to the island.

I'm mistaken, Janice thought. *Matthew Ward wasn't here last night. The stranger just looks a lot like him. Yes, that's all it is. Remember the guy who spent seven years in prison for theft, and then they found the real criminal, and he looked a lot like him? Yes, his doppelganger! Besides, a guy like Matthew Ward would never do something so horrible.*

Nevertheless, as she stared at the photo, her mind screamed, *he was here last night, it was him, it was him*, but she shook her head, refusing to give her memories an audience. However, her memories fought back by refusing to remove the memories of the night from the forefront of her thoughts, and suddenly, she froze as a particular memory gripped her – the gun. *Where is the gun?*

"The gun," she whispers, "I think the gun dropped out of his pants pocket."

She searched her mind, remembering a sound when the stranger dropped his pants on the ground, *but how could it have fallen out of his pants pocket?*

Her thoughts travelled to when her toe was throbbing. She didn't stomp it on anything between the bed and door because nothing was there. She searched her mind some more. She remembered springing from the bed to lock the door; after she'd locked it, she felt her toe throbbing. She glanced in the direction of her mother's room, wondering if she'd found it when she'd cleaned up her bedroom last night.

No, she would have said something if she did, Janice thought, *and besides, the gun was in his pants pocket. He would have heard it if it had fallen out when he was rushing to get dressed.*

Nevertheless, she folded the newspaper and placed it under the small, dark brown, oval table in front of her. She stood and headed for her bedroom. She briefly hesitated at the opened door, but taking a deep breath, she squared her shoulders and entered the room, holding her head high. Janice locked the door and stood surveyed the room. Then, stooping, she looked under the bed. It was very dark under there, partly due to the numerous plastic bags filled with her parents' things.

She stood, then lifted the spring-filled mattress into the air. Her eyes searched among the bags. Her hands grew tired quickly, and just as they were buckling under the weight, there it was, sandwiched between two orange and white supermarket plastic bags. She slowly lowered the mattress onto its base, then, lying on her belly, she crawled a little under the bed. She pushed away a few of the bags in front of her before stretching out her hand into the area where she saw the gun. She found it quickly and slowly wrapped her fingers around it. She slowly pushed herself out from under the bed. Then, with the weapon in her hand, she sat on the floor and looked at it. Janice's hands shook, and the small firearm almost fell out of it.

The gun was black with two silver lines on both sides and slightly larger than the palm of her hands.

She slowly rubbed the weapon. Her hands trembled again. She briefly closed her eyes, and her mind formulated several ideas. She sighed, and then turning around, she carefully rested the gun on the bed before walking over to the chest of draws and quietly pushing it a little away from its spot. Then, stooping down, Janice quietly lifted a board from the floor. Then, turning to the chest of drawers, she pulled open a bottom drawer.

"Where is it?" she quietly asked, searching through the clothing.

Oh yeah, Mom repacked my things last night. I forgot.

She closed the drawer and searched through two more before finding what she wanted. Then she picked up the gun and wrapped it in the wash cloth. She replaced the board and pushed back the chest of draws.

Her eyes rested on the pillow and sheet on the floor, and she walked over to them and picked them up. She took another deep breath before turning and walking to the bed. She dropped them on it. She stood looking at the bed for a few seconds before turning around and slowly lowering her body into a sitting position.

Janice sat on the edge of the bed but immediately jumped up. She grabbed a pillow from the bed and buried her face in it. Janice screamed and screamed some more until her screams turned into unstoppable tears, and she lowered herself to the ground and stayed there until her tears stopped falling. Then, after wiping her face with her hands, she slowly rose to her feet and left the bedroom.

"Mommy," she called, knocking on her mother's bedroom door.

"What is it?" was the instant reply.

"I don't want to go to the police station today. I want to put this behind me and move on."

Janice rested her right ear on the bedroom door, waiting for her mother's reply, but nothing came.

"Mommy?"

A loud sigh escaped from behind the door.

"Just do whatever you want," her mother called out angrily.

Janice's shoulders collapsed in sadness and relief before turning and returning to her bedroom.

As she locked the door inside the room, a deep need to drown out her thoughts overwhelmed her, and she remembered her Walkman. Her eyes darted to the dresser, hoping to find it there. She hoped her mother had found it and placed it there, but it was not there. Her eyes darted around the room before she thought, *It must have fallen between the wall and the bed when I tried to flip the mattress.*

She slowly and quietly pulled the bed frame from the wall and found the Walkman. It was between a plastic bag and the wall. She carefully picked it up and examined it, and to her relief, it was undamaged.

"Thank God," she whispered, holding it close to her chest as she exhaled quietly.

The weekend went by slowly for Janice, and she refused to go outside, and to her surprise, her mother said nothing about it. She also spent most of that time in her room.

Monday finally rolled around, and still, she did not want to leave the house. However, on Sunday, her mother made it clear that she was going to school, and it was not up for debate. So, she went to school, and on that day and the rest of the week, she buried herself in school activities, and on several occasions, she found her best friend, Nicki, staring at her.

"Is everything alright?" Nicki asked throughout the week.

"Yes, sure, everything's fine," Janice replied, smiling broadly and exposing her dimples.

When she missed her period the following month, she didn't think much about it because she was accustomed to it. Her monthly periods were more irregular than they were regular. However, she was surprised when her mother asked her about her period. She could not remember the last day her mother asked her about it. Nevertheless, she told her, and her mother immediately announced, "I'm taking you to see a doctor."

Janice opened her mouth to object, but the look on her mother's face told her to keep quiet, so she did. So, two days later, on Friday, she missed school and was given a urine test at a doctor's office, and the doctor said to her mother, "Yes, she is pregnant."

Janice's heart fell to her feet, and she sank lower and lower in the grey armless chair in the doctor's office. She willed the ground to open and engulf her.

This can't be happening. This can't be happening, Janice chanted, trying to drown out her mother's and the doctor's voices.

She continued to chant as she walked home with her mother. She hardly noticed the automobiles, horse-drawn buggies, and other activities around her.

"I know someone who can take care of it," her mother said, wiping sweat from her forehead with the back of her hand.

Janice nodded, even though she didn't hear what her mother said.

"We will have to do it right away, but I don't have enough money, so I'll have to borrow the rest," she continued.

Janice nodded again, still lost in her mind.

They continued home with her mother speaking and Janice nodding but hearing nothing. They returned home, and Janice carefully lowered her body into the single sitter chair and looked across the room at her mother, who was now sitting at the dining room table with her back to her. She had started to sort the day's mail. The delivery worker had dropped them through an opened louvres window while they were out.

"Mommy, what am I going to do?" Janice asked, "I can't have a baby now. I'm only sixteen."

Her mother slowly turned in the chair to look at her.

"Weren't you listening to me when I was talking?" she asked as frown lines deepened across her forehead.

"Kind of."

Her mother shook her head several times before returning to the day's mail on the table.

"I know someone who can take care of it," she said over her shoulders.

"What do you mean?"

"I'm talking about Mama Taitt. She took care of it for Justine and can do it for you, too, but we must act quickly. Before I go to work today, I'll stop by her house and talk to her.

"Justine, Justine. Who's Justine?"

Then, like a hundred-meter sprinter, Justine sprinted to the forefront of her mind. Yes, sixteen-year-old Justine was pregnant with her boyfriend's child, and Mama Taitt, a retired midwife, helped her abort the baby. Well, at least that was what the gossip mill said, and it happened about three years ago.

"No." Even before she fully formed the word in her mind, Janice heard herself saying.

"No, what?" her mother asked, getting out of the chair.

She headed for the kitchen.

"No, I'm not going to kill this baby," she clarified, looking down at her trembling hands.

"What are you saying? Are you crazy, girl? Why am I wasting my money and time sending you to school? It's a fetus, not a baby. Therefore, you wouldn't be killing anyone."

"No," Janice said, shaking her head, "I'm not going to do it."

Although a large woman, her mother was exceptionally light on her feet, and before Janice could lift her head from her trembling hand, her mother changed direction from the kitchen and bolted like lightning toward her. She stood over her like an angry bear.

"You listen to me, little girl, there's only one woman in this house, and I'm it. You'll do what I say. You will get an abortion, and that's final." Her voice rose as she stabbed her finger through the air at her.

"I can't do it. This baby hasn't done anything wrong," Janice meekly protested.

"Do you want to ruin your life? Is that what you want?" she spat out.

"We can put the baby up for adoption," Janice looked at her.

"You are a waste, girl! Just a waste!" her mother yelled.

Janice looked down at her hands and stretched out her lips.

Her mother slapped her across the face.

The slap stunned and paralyzed her for a few seconds. Janice looked up at her mother and saw that another slap was coming. She scrambled out of the chair. She was almost out of her mother's reach when she grabbed her by the neck of her yellow T-shirt. Her mother spun her around to face her and slapped her again.

"You think I'm foolish?" she shouted in her face. "I know what happened between you and some guy in this house!"

Janice raised her hand to protect her face from another slap, and she succeeded.

"You better start telling me the truth, girl," her mother said, shaking her before pushing her away. Janice fell backwards into another chair.

"What do you mean?" Her face was wearing a mask of fear.

"For starters, you wouldn't go to the police, and now you wouldn't have an abortion?" her mother said, towering over her with her hands folded across her breast.

"Abortion is killing and..."

"Stop playing games with me, girl!"

Her mother unfolded her arms, and Janice sunk more into the chair, trying to protect her face and stomach.

"Did you bring some boy into my house, and things got out of hand?" Janice's mom asked, glaring at her.

Janice opened her mouth, but no words came out. She slammed it shut. She shook her head and bit her lower lip.

"Someone broke in here and attacked me. The police don't care, and you know that. The cops took three days to get to Jeff after those thieves broke into his house, which only happened about two weeks before this happened to me. The police don't care, and everybody knows that." Janice fought to keep her voice from trembling.

Her mother continued to look at her before she began to rock slowly back and forth on her feet—a telltale sign of her thinking. Janice decided to make a run for it. She inched away from her mother's legs and fled from the chair to stand behind the single-seater chair to separate them.

"All I want to do is just keep the baby until he is born and then give him up for adoption," Janice said sulkily.

Her mother launched for her, but Janice backed away.

"What's wrong with you?" Janice asked.

"What's wrong with me? What's wrong with me?" her mother roared. "Who do you think you are? Who do you think you're talking to?"

Janice said nothing but slightly bent her head.

"I had a deadbeat husband and two fools for children," her mother declared, shaking her head.

"My brother and I may be fools, but at least he was smart enough to leave you and this dump."

"Get out, get out, get out!" her mother yelled, launching for her again, "You ungrateful, rude child, get out, just get out of my house."

Janice continued to avoid her.

"Get out!" her mother yelled, pointing at the door.

Suddenly, three loud knocks sounded on the front door. Janice jumped, and they both turned to stare at the door. The knocks came again.

"Who is it?" her mother called, trying to

control her breathing.

"It's me, Thomas," a deep, slow voice replied.

Thomas, Thomas, Thomas. Who is Thomas? Janice wondered.

The voice sounded familiar, but she could not place it. Janice saw recognition on her mother's face as her mouth suddenly but briefly fell open.

"Thomas, who?" Janice called out to the knocker.

"It's me, Jan," the voice said. "It's me, Teddy Bear."

A kaleidoscope of emotions burst in her heart, and it travelled to her head, and Janice staggered a few steps backwards. She quickly regained her balance, and before she knew it, she covered the distance between her and the door, and after unlocking and flinging it open, Janice froze on its threshold as she stared at the person in front of her. Thomas was standing in front of her.

Thomas was now a tall, stocky man instead of the tall, skinny boy she remembered. His curly hair was cut low, and he had a short goatee. His red and white T-shirt was in his long blue jeans, and his black and white low-top athletic shoes looked new.

"Hi, Jan," he said, smiling broadly.

Her eyes grew large, and a huge smile engulfed her face.

"What are you doing here?" their mother boomed behind her.

"Hi, Mom," Thomas said, as his eyes briefly travelled from Janice to their mother before returning to Janice.

He opened his arms, and Janice stepped into them. They held each other tightly.

"You're not welcome here," their mother said.

Janice and Thomas slowly released each other.

"Yeah, I know, I remember," Thomas said, looking past Janice to their mother.

"What are you talking about?" Janice asked. She turned around to look at her. "This is Thomas, your son and my brother."

"He's not welcome here," she repeated.

"It's okay, Jan," Thomas said. "If you have some time, we can go for a walk to the beach."

"She's not leaving this house," their mother said, folding her arms across her breast.

"What are you talking about?" Janice asked, frowning, "A few minutes ago, you were yelling at me to leave, and now you want me to stay?"

"I'm finished. I'm done. Do whatever you want," her mom replied, throwing her hands into the air and turning away. She disappeared into the house.

CHAPTER 6
HE LEFT

A short time later, Janice and Thomas sat on a large grey rock.

They were on Brown's Beach, a brown sandy beach within walking distance of her home. They sat silently and occasionally threw pebbles into the calm, sky-blue waters. When they were younger and were allowed to go to the beach, they would pick up small stones along the way. When they arrived, they would compete to see who could throw a pebble the farthest in the water. Today, a lump of small stones lay between them as they sat on the rock.

"I won," Janice said suddenly, her face beaming.

Thomas' mouth fell open in mock surprise, and Janice burst into laughter. His mouth opened even wider before he, too, burst out laughing.

Although Thomas was nine years older than her, their physical resemblance was remarkable. They shared their father's thick eyebrows, long eyelashes, high cheekbones, and broad, flat noses. They shared their mother's height and complexion, but their eyes and dimples were theirs. Yet, somehow, they resembled their parents and each other.

When they stopped laughing, Janice surveyed the almost deserted beach while shaking a few pebbles, like a shak-shak, in her left hand. A man, a woman, and a white Akita dog were jogging close to the shoreline. A few white herons were also strolling along the edge of the water. They were picking at things that Janice could not see. In the distance, three colourful fishing boats were bopping lazily on the water. No one was in them.

"Why did you leave me with her, Teddy Bear?" Janice asked, looking down at the pebbles in her hand.

Thomas was throwing a pebble when she spoke, and his hand faltered for a few seconds, but he completed the action by throwing the small rock into the water. Janice watched as it dropped on the shoreline, and seconds later, the salt-filled water boldly covered it before withdrawing from the coastline. Thomas cleared his throat.

"I'm sorry I left you behind, Jan. I did it because I was selfish. I was only thinking about myself. I couldn't bear living at home with Mom anymore, so I kept thinking about how to get away from her and this place."

Janice's shoulders shook slightly, and unexpectedly, tears filled her eyes and rolled down her cheeks. Thomas placed his long arm around her shoulders, and tears tumbled out of her.

"Shhh... It's okay. It's okay," he whispered, as his tears threatened him, "I'm here now. I'm here now."

The breeze blew over her body as Janice continued to cry. She cried and cried, and when she thought she could not cry anymore, fresh tears rolled down her cheeks. Thomas took a light blue and white handkerchief from his back pants pocket and handed it to her. She wiped away the tears and the cold running out of her nose.

"I'm a little better now," Janice said, exhaling loudly as her shoulders involuntarily slumped.

Thomas kissed her on the head before removing his hand from around her shoulders.

"I couldn't stay at home anymore," Thomas said. "I was going crazy there. Mom and I were always quarrelling, and we were quarrelling about any and every little thing. A week didn't go by without her hitting me. I couldn't take it anymore." He paused, lost in his world of memories. "I was so afraid that I would lose it and hit her back one day. I just had to get out of there. I just had to leave."

"Oh," Janice said, looking at him, "I didn't realize it was that bad for you."

"Mom used to say, 'You're good for nothing. You're just like your father, worthless.'"

"Yeah, I remember that part," Janice said, nodding.

"The day that I left home, things had gotten terrible. I cursed her and told her I would never again set foot back in that house," Thomas said, picking up a pebble from the small pile beside him.

He pelted it forcefully, and Janice barely saw it drop into the water. Janice cleared her throat.

"The day you left, Mom didn't come to pick me up from school. The vice-principal had to drive me home," she said.

The couple with the dog was now retracing their steps, and instead of running, they were briskly walking. The dog was still running, though.

"When I got home, Mom answered the door and told the vice-principal she'd sent you to pick me up."

"I was long gone by then," Thomas said, staring into the sea.

"Yeah, I know because after the vice-principal left, Mom told me you were selfish, and because of your selfishness, you left home, and you weren't coming back," Janice said, throwing a pebble. "I didn't believe her, though, and I told her so. I thought she'd thrown you out or something like that."

Thomas exhaled heavily.

"For the longest time, I refused to believe you would willingly leave me behind. Where did you go? What happened to you?" Janice asked.

Thomas took a deep breath before answering. "When I left home, I walked and hitched a ride over to Somerset, and for the first week, I slept in an abandoned theatre with some other people. I didn't have enough money to rent a place."

"You were homeless?" Janice asked, surprised.

"Yeah," he said, rubbing behind his head, "I needed a job, so I went looking for one, but I couldn't find anything permanent. I would get a few hours of work in the street markets, though. I had to carry boxes of vegetables and so on for the vendors, and I was happy for the jobs, but they didn't always pay in cash."

"They didn't? How else were you paid?"

"They would give me food in exchange."

"Oh."

"Yeah, but then I met a guy who had a farm, and he provided housing for anyone who worked on his farm."

"Really?" Janice asked.

"Yeah, some farmers do that, but I went

to Somerset because I heard that there was a construction boom there, but none of the sites I checked were hiring, so I went on the farm."

"Did you like it there?"

"It was alright. I worked there for about a year, and then I met this guy looking for carpenters to work for him. So, by this time, I had more than enough money to rent a place, so I left and went to work for this guy, and I am still working for him."

"Wow," Janice said, "I'm glad it all worked out."

As she spoke, her mind struggled to find something, something that was at the corner of her mind, but every time she turned to look at it, it disappeared. She shook her head, and as she looked down to pick up a pebble, her brother's left hand was resting on the rock, and suddenly, the thing that was out of her view became visible, and her eyes darted to his face with her mouth opened.

"Did you get married, Thomas?" she exclaimed.

A broad smile spread across his face as he replied. "Yes, I am married. You have a sister-in-law and will soon become an aunt."

A broad smile spread across her face, and she threw her arms around him. "Oh, Teddy Bear, congratulations."

"Thanks," he said, returning her hug.

"Tell me about her. Where did the two of you meet? When did you get married? When will the baby be born? Wow!" Janice asked, releasing him.

"Whoa, one question at a time," Thomas said, raising his hands as if to defend himself as he leaned away from her. He laughed.

"Do you have a photo of her?"

"I certainly do," he said, pushing his right hand into his jeans' back pocket and pulling out a black leather wallet.

He flipped it open, pulled a photo out, and handed it to her.

The colour photo was a headshot of a broadly smiling, teeth-shown, bright-eyed woman. Her curly hair passed her shoulders, and pink and blue flowers surrounded her.

"She's beautiful, Teddy," Janice said, slowly returning the photo to him. "When will I get to meet her?" She smiled at him.

"Soon, very soon," he replied, smiling down at the photo before returning it to his wallet.

"I can't wait. How did the two of you meet?"

"Well," he said, "We met about three years ago, and our first wedding anniversary was four months ago."

"Congratulations."

"Thanks. ..., we met when I was working on a house next to her home."

"Hmm, I see. You were picking up girls on the job."

Thomas laughed, and Janice joined in.

"Yeah. Something like that, and the rest is history, as they say."

"Cool," Janice said, "I can't wait to meet her."

"She can't wait to meet you, too."

"Did you guys have a big wedding?"

Thomas studied her face for a few seconds as she bit down on her lower lip.

"I wanted you to be there, Jan, but I didn't think it was fair for me to turn up after all those years with just an invitation to my wedding."

Janice nodded and gazed out into the sea.

A brief silence passed between them before Thomas asked, "Jan, what's going on with you and Mom?"

The faraway gaze remained on her face as she picked up the last pebble and held it in her right palm. She took a deep breath before slowly letting it out.

"Someone broke into the house and attacked me, and now I'm pregnant. Mom wants me to kill the baby, but I can't. I wouldn't do it."

Several seconds of silence fell between them before Thomas exclaimed, "What?"
He jumped off the boulder and stood with

his hands on his hips, looking at her. Tears danced in her eyes, but she rapidly blinked them away as fresh cold entered her nostrils, and she sniffled.

"Oh, Jan!" Thomas exclaimed as his hands flew from his hips to the sides of his head. He started to pace in front of her.

"And I know who it is, but no one will believe me even if I tell them who it is. Mom doesn't even believe that someone broke in." Janice looked down at the pebble in her hand.

"What?" he asked as he stopped pacing, and his hands fell from his head and landed at his sides.

Janice sniffled again.

"Mom was at work," she began, telling him the entire story and ending with when he came knocking on the front door.

The sun began to play peek-a-boo in the clouds, and the water was receding into the sea, but Janice took no notice of them.

"And that's about it," she said.

"Let me get this straight. This guy thought that you hired him to attack you?" Thomas asked.

"Well, that's how it seems to me. That's the only thing that makes sense in this dark, twisted scheme."

"Yes, this is dark and twisted. Why would anyone, especially a rich guy, do something like this? What kind of messed-up thing is this?"

"I haven't given this much thought, but I'm considering asking his parents for help. I'm not going to tell them how the baby got here. I just want them to find a good home for the baby," Janice said quietly.

"What! You need to go to the police station so that they can put him behind bars."

"No! No one will believe me." Fear edged the corners of her voice.

"I'm someone, and I believe you, and besides, it's their job to investigate a report even if they don't believe it."

Janice went quiet for a few minutes, and her brother waited for her to see sense in what he had said.

"Mom wants me to put this behind me and move on, and I've tried. I'm working hard at school, but now I'm pregnant, and I can't keep pretending that what happened didn't happen. I want to talk to his parents. I won't tell them that he…, he attacked me. I'll just tell them the baby is his, and they can get a blood test to confirm it. This way, they'll be more willing to help me."

Unexpectedly, tears returned to her eyes, but she blinked them away and said, "I'm too young to have a baby, and even if I wasn't, I couldn't love a baby that came from me in this way, but I'm not going to hurt the baby either."

Distant screams of excitement suddenly travelled to their ears, and Janice slowly turned to look over her shoulder, and she saw a group of children running and laughing as they raced towards the sea. *School's out already*, she thought before turning back to Thomas.

"Wait a minute," she said, "how come you're here right now? I'm usually at school during the time you come."

"Yeah, I know," he said, "I stopped at your school, and before you ask how I know which secondary school you're attending, I found out a little while back from an old schoolmate whose brother is at the same school."

"Oh."

"Your principal, as you might know, taught me in elementary school, and she told me that you called in sick today."

"Oh," she said and lapsed into silence before speaking again. "Mom is always forcing me to go to church, and now she's telling me it's okay to kill an innocent baby. I can't do it, Teddy. I wouldn't do it!"

Janice clenched her teeth and sighed heavily.

"It's getting late. We better start heading back," Janice said, slowly getting on her feet.

"Is Mom still working as a security

guard?"

"She is, and she'll be going in for six o'clock today. If she hasn't left already, she'll be leaving home soon, but I have my house key, so I'm not worried about getting back home before she leaves."

Janice pulled a gold chain from around her neck and showed him the attached key.

"Okay," Thomas said, falling into steps with her, and they started to retrace their steps to her home.

"I'm so scared, Teddy," Janice rubbed her forehead. "Everything is going relatively alright one day, and I'm waking up in this nightmare the next day. I don't deserve this."

"Pack all your things, clothes, books, whatever you want, and I'll be back at nine o'clock tomorrow morning to take you with me."

She stopped walking.

"What... what do you mean?" she asked, "I don't understand."

"Amanda and I want you to come and live with us. I came to ask Mom if she would allow you to come and live with us, but we were thinking of you coming at the end of the school year."

"Really?" Janice asked as fear and excitement fought within her.

"That's if it's okay with you, too," he quickly added.

"If that's okay with me? Of course, it's okay with me!" She hugged him.

"Do you think Mom will say yes to you coming with me tomorrow?" he asked after they started walking again.

"On one hand, she's putting me out, and on the next hand, ..." Janice threw her hands into the air.

They walked silently for the rest of their journey, and when they got to her home, their mother was not there. Thomas stood outside and waited for her to check the windows and the kitchen door. They were securely locked. Afterwards, they talked outside for a few more minutes, and when she went inside and locked the door, he left.

Janice was sad to see her big brother leave, but his promise to return the following day made her happy. She smiled. Besides, she had to pack and didn't have much time. Janice speed-walked to the kitchen, pulled open a brown overhead cupboard and took out three large black garbage bags. She then hurried to her bedroom and locked the door.

CHAPTER 7
GOODBYE

Janice looked around her bedroom for a few seconds before deciding where to start.

She walked over to the dresser and picked up everything on top of it before dropping them in a black bag. Janice pulled open the drawers and transferred her folded clothes and other items into the same bag. She continued packing, and sometime later, three large black plastic bags were full of her belongings. She giggled before slowly lowering herself onto the floor.

She sat on the floor, lost in her thoughts, until the sound of her empty stomach entered her ears.

I should get up and get something to eat, Janice thought, but as soon as the last word left her thoughts, she fell asleep on the floor, which had become her bed.

Janice awoke around five o'clock the following morning, and her body was aching everywhere. Her stomach growled loudly.

"I'm so hungry," she whispered. "I feel as though I haven't eaten in days."

She sat up on the floor, and after a few minutes, she slowly stood and surveyed the bedroom. The bedroom light was still on.

All my things are in these garbage bags, but this room still looks the same. It seems as though I've never been here. Janice's stomach growled again. *I better get something to eat right now before I hurt the baby, but I'll need to shower first.*

As she showered, she hoped her mother did not hear the running water.

After showering, she wore a white T-shirt and long blue jeans. She lightly brushed her cornrowed hair and then headed for the kitchen. Janice tiptoed around the kitchen, trying not to wake her mother.

"Not bad, not bad, if I do say so myself," she whispered, complimenting herself for how quietly she was moving in the kitchen.

She smiled as she poured steaming oatmeal porridge into a large white cup before turning and heading for the dining room. As she did, she almost dropped the cup.

Her mother stood at the kitchen entrance with her arms folded across her chest. She was wearing her long blue and white floral sleeping dress. The sleeping gown almost touched the floor.

"I... I... didn't mean to wake you up,"

she mumbled, lowering her eyes as she tried to gain control of her pounding heart and trembling hands.

Her mother did not reply. Janice started walking towards her, leaving the kitchen, but her mother did not attempt to move out of her way.

"Excuse me, please," Janice mumbled, avoiding looking directly at her.

Her mother blocked the passageway for a few more seconds before slowly throwing her hips from side to side as she walked into the kitchen. Janice walked over to the dining table and, with her hands still shaking, tried to put the cup down without spilling the porridge. She was thankful that she did not fill the cup to the top. None of it spilled. She sat down, prayed, and then broke unsalted crackers into the cup of oatmeal. She stirred it slowly before taking a spoonful, blowing it, and putting it into her mouth.

"Where's your brother living?" her mother asked. She was in the kitchen pouring porridge into a big floral teacup.

"I don't know," Janice glanced at the heart-shaped clock on the wall.

"Didn't he tell you where he's living?" she asked, her voice filled with disbelief as she walked over to the dining table.

"No." Janice still chewed on her food.

"Why did he come here?" Janice's mom

put the cup to her mouth.

"He came to see how I was doing," Janice said, with her mouth still full of food.

"I see."

A few minutes of silence passed between them, and Janice glanced at the clock again, and it said that two minutes had passed since she last looked at it. It was now six-thirty. Some fowl cocks crowded outside.

"Do you have somewhere to go?" her mother asked.

Janice pretended not to hear her by looking at and rubbing her upper left arm as though something had bitten her.

"I talked with Mama Fay yesterday, and she can come by on Tuesday. You will have to stay home from school for a few days afterwards," her mother continued, looking at her over her cup.

Janice frowned and bit down on her lower lip.

"Are you going to pretend you didn't hear that, too?"

"I heard you," Janice said, nodding and putting the last spoonful of food into her mouth.

"So, no back talk about killing?" she asked, her voice mocking.

"No," Janice said, chewing her food.

"Did you tell your brother about the attack?"

"Yes."

Janice still did not meet her mother's eyes as she pushed the chair back and got up.

"I have something to do in my room, Mom."

"More packing to do?" she asked, lifting her left eyebrow.

Janice froze, but the fowl cocks continued their waking call.

"Don't be so surprised," her mother said as a large smile spread across her face and laughter danced in her eyes.

Janice fell back into the chair.

"But you don't know your brother as I do, but you will find out soon."

"What, what do you mean?" Janice frowned.

"What time did he say he would be coming for you?"

"At nine?"

"He's not coming. He's just like your father. They never keep their word. He took off and left me here to struggle with the two of you," she spits out.

Janice's shoulders stiffened. "He's going to come," she said.

"Wait and see for yourself."

"You wait, and you'll see. He's going to come," Janice's hand shook slightly, the spoon in the cup jumped, and her shoulders slumped slightly.

"Wake me up at eleven," her mother said, getting up and heading for the kitchen. She placed her cup in the silver sink and returned to her bedroom.

"He's not going to come. He's just like your father. They never keep their word," Janice quietly mocked as she got up from the table and walked into the kitchen. She washed their dishes and then returned to her bedroom.

Janice intended to read a book in her bedroom while waiting for her brother, but she drifted off to sleep. Sometime later, she awoke in a panic and struggled to keep her eye open as she raised her hand to look at her digital watch. She struggled to keep her eyes focused on the numbers, and when she succeeded, she read ten fifty. Janice jumped up from the floor and rushed to the front door.

Did I miss him knocking? If I did, he might have left a note at the door.

She looked down at the door for a note but found nothing. She opened the door, stepped outside, and searched the street for a few minutes. She did not see her brother coming or going. She closed the door and moved to a louvres window, where she could see farther down the street. She stared as far down as she could but did not see him.

"Please come," she quietly pleaded.

She waited a few more minutes, but the street remained empty. Then, with a heavy heart, she sighed and turned away from the window. She went to knock on her mother's bedroom door.

"So, you're still here. I told you your brother wouldn't come," her mother said after showering and dressing in a blue pleated, broad shoulder strap dress.

Janice was sitting in the living room, still holding on to the hope that her brother would knock on the door any second now.

"He came here yesterday, dressed up and filled your head with nonsense. He may look different, but he's still the same, useless," she continued before bursting into laughter.

Janice's head suddenly felt full, and for a second, she felt unsteady. Her right hand folded into a fist as she watched and listened to her mother's laughter.

"How can you say things like that? He's your son!"

"Useless," she repeated as she continued to laugh.

Suddenly, three loud but rapid knocks come on the front door. Janice jumped. She exchanged a glance with her mother, and for a moment, Janice thought she saw a flicker of fear walking across her mother's eyes, but it quickly disappeared. Janice shook her head, jumped out of the chair, and hurried to the door. She flung it open and found Thomas standing there with a sheepish smile. He was dressed in blue jeans and a blue T-shirt.

"Sorry, Sis," he said.

Janice smiled broadly.

"My boss called me late last night. He needed me to come in early this morning because of an emergency. I couldn't finish the job in time to get here for nine, and yesterday I forgot to ask you for the house phone number. I tried the one we had when I lived here, but it is not in service anymore."

"Yeah, we changed it years ago," Janice said, still smiling.

"On the bright side, though, I get to use my boss's jeep, so we don't have to call a taxi."

She hugged him.

"Where's Mom?" he asked after they'd parted.

"She's right here," Janice said, turning to look at their mother, but she was gone.

Her eyes scanned the house for her, but she couldn't find her.

"She probably went back to her bedroom," Janice concluded.

"Go and get her for me, please."

"Yeah, sure," Janice said and headed for the bedroom.

The door was closed, so after knocking on it, Janice said, "Mom, Thomas is outside and wants to talk to you."

No answer came.

"Mom?" Janice called, knocking harder on the door.

"Go!" her muffled voice yelled out.

"What?"

"And leave my key on the table."

Janice didn't reply but stood there silently for a few seconds.

"Bye, Mom," she quietly called out.

She hesitated for a few seconds, hoping to hear a response, but she slowly backed away from the door when nothing came. Then, shrugging, she turned and hurried to her bedroom. She grabbed two of the black garbage bags and rushed back to Thomas.

"She's not coming out. She told me to go and to leave the key on the table," Janice told him.

"Yes, I heard her," Thomas said, taking the bags from her. "Are you okay?"

"Yeah, sure," Janice replied as unexpected tears filled her eyes. "I have one more bag." Janice quietly turned away so he would not see the tears in her eyes.

"Okay. I'll put these in the jeep."

Janice rushed to the bedroom and grabbed the remaining bag as she wiped her tears. She momentarily paused as she looked at her mother's still-closed door and quietly whispered, "Take care of yourself, Mom."

She stopped at the dining room and removed the gold chain from around her neck. She then pulled the silver key from it and placed it on the table. She looked around the house, and more tears entered her eyes, but she quickly blinked them away.

"Are you ready?" Thomas asked.

"Yes," she said, the words catching in her throat, "I'm ready."

"It's okay. Everything will be okay."

"Okay."

She walked to the door, and her brother took the bag from her. She slammed the door shut and listened for the lock to slip into place, and it did. She knew that by closing it loudly, their mother would realize they had left.

CHAPTER 8
AT WORK

The following morning, when James awoke, he was surprised to find his mom in the kitchen, and she was buttering toasted bread.

"Mom? Morning," he greeted.

She looked up from the toast, and a huge smile covered her face.

He searched her face for signs of the night before but saw none.

"Good morning, sweetheart."

He walked over to her and, slightly bending, kissed her on the forehead.

"Had a good sleep?" she asked, adding two more toast to the plate with four other toasts.

"It was alright," he replied, shrugging. "How about you? Are you okay?"

"Me? Yes, I'm fine," she replied, buttering the toast.

"Good. Because you weren't looking too well last night."

As he spoke, he reached up and pulled

open the white-painted door of an overhead cupboard. He took down two medium-sized teacups.

"I know," she said, "but don't worry about me. Everything will be okay."

She picked up the toast and plate full of scrambled eggs and headed for the dining room.

"What was wrong?" he asked, following her with teacups and a teapot from the counter.

"Nothing this old body can't handle," Janice placed the dishes on the table.

With that, James knew that his mother would no longer talk about it. They ate at the dining table after praying over the food.

"What's the name of the magazine you'll be working at again?" she asked, "I forget what you said."

"It's called Glen's Magazine."

"And when do you start?" Janice looked down at her plate.

"They want me to come in on Monday." He swallowed a mouthful of tea.

"I guess the timing for both of these jobs is working out well," she said before biting into a toast.

"Yeah, God is good." James nodded. "I leave one job and start another."

They chit-chatted throughout breakfast, and afterwards, James, after taking a shower, quickly dressed in the bike store's dark blue T-shirt and long black jeans. He kissed his mom goodbye and rushed out of the house to catch the seven o'clock, government-owned bus.

Mom is so right about these two jobs working out so well, James thought as he sat in the yellow and white bus, waiting for it to pull away from the curb.

He was working temporarily at the bike shop. One of the shop's permanent staff was on vacation, and James was filling in for him. Now that the staff's holiday was ending, this would make it his last week there. He enjoys working at the shop, and when the boss suggested keeping him on for the third Saturday of the month, he jumped at the opportunity. The bike shop was usually busy during that time, and they typically needed some extra hands, and he was more than happy to continue there.

However, the new job was permanent, and the pay rate was higher than the pay at the bike shop, but having both cheques would come in handy.

University, here I come, he thought as a smile crossed his lips. However, the smile did not last long because his mind shifted to his mom. He was troubled by her sudden illness and speedy recovery. *What's going on with her?*

He took a deep breath and closed his eyes for the rest of the journey.

For James, the rest of the week went by quickly, and he was relieved when his mom did not get sick again. Still, something was troubling her, and she would not talk to him about it, and he could not place his fingers on what it could be. He thought it might have to do with her job, but he was unsure.

The following Monday, at eight a.m., he sat in the receptionist's area at Glen's Magazine. The receptionist was sitting behind a semi-circle desk at the opposite side of the door's entrance. There were seven doors to her left, and on her right, there were three doors, and directly behind her, there was one door. The doors were all painted in cream; the job title tags were on some, while the name tags were on four. Most of the doors were closed, while the others were slightly ajar.
He was interviewed at a job fair three weeks ago, so this was his first time inside the building.

The building was quiet.

Wow, James thought, looking around him. He was waiting for the receptionist to finish using the telephone.

I thought it would be a lot noisier in here.

The receptionist put down the receiver and called his name. She motioned with her hand for him to come closer to her. As he approached her, she stood and walked around the large desk. She wore a navy blue pantsuit and a white inside shirt. A name tag was affixed to her chest's left side, and it read Alicia Jones. Her body was well proportioned, and her black shoulder-length and straightened hair curled at the nape of her neck. James judged her to be in her early fifties.

"Follow me, please," she said, turning left.

She took him to the first door on the left, and after knocking on it, she waited for a few seconds before turning the doorknob and pushing it open.

The room was small but large enough to hold two black-painted computer desks at its centre. The desks faced each other, and both had cream computer monitors and keyboards. Paper folders were also on the desks. At the back of the room, three grey filing cabinets were sitting in the left corner of the wall, and there was also a medium-sized built-in bookshelf with several books on it.

A dark-skinned man dressed in long brown pants and a long white-sleeved shirt was sitting at one of the desks, and he was typing. James judged him to be about thirty years old. He stopped typing and introduced himself as Simon, and after some instructions from Mrs. Jones, he sat opposite Simon and turned on the computer.

"How long have you been here?" James asked as he waited for the computer to set up.

"Look," Simon said, without looking away from the file in front of him, "I don't mean to be rude, but I need to get this work done before my first break, so I don't have any time to talk."

"Okay," James said, smiling slightly and raising his hand in surrender, "you're all about the work, and I'm with you on that."

The computer was now ready to be used, and James opened the first file on his desk and began his first day as a copy typist at Glen's Magazine.

As the day progressed, he met a few more staff members who brought work for Simon and him to store on the computer, and this was the routine for the rest of the week.

On Friday, after returning to work from his lunch break, the receptionist, Mrs. Jones, stopped him by raising her hand and motioning him to her. She was on the telephone, so he stood at her desk and waited for her to finish. She wore a striped black and blue pantsuit, and her hair was like a bun in the center of her head.

"James," she said, after putting down the receiver, "Mr. Ward would like to see you in his office at one-thirty."

She handed him a sticky note, which

said, "Mr. Ward's office at one-thirty." James' heart skipped a beat, and he swallowed hard, thanked her and went to his office.

What did I do wrong? he wondered as he entered his office. *Am I going to get fired?*

When he entered, Simon was in the room and immediately got up from behind his desk.

"See you in an hour," he said and left, closing the door behind him.

James sat at his desk, and as he began typing, his mind continued to dwell on his one-thirty appointment. His boss, also the magazine owner, wanted to see him.

Is he going to fire me?

"Help me, O Lord," he silently prayed.

He shook his head as though trying to clear his mind, and after performing a few hand stretches, his fingers flew across the keyboard, and he became lost in the articles he was storing on the computer. Time quickly flew by, and at twenty-seven minutes after one, he left his working area and headed for Mr. Oliver Ward's office. His office was the room that was directly behind the receptionist's desk.

He knocked on the cream-painted door with Mr. Ward's name on it.

"Come in," a deep voice commanded.

James swallowed before stretching out his hand and turning the silver doorknob.

He pushed it open and entered the room.

Mr. Ward was sitting behind a rectangular, dark-stained cherry oak desk, and he rose from his chair and walked around the desk as James approached him. He was a tall, dark-skinned man with curly, low-cut hair, and it was evident that he was balding. Mr. Ward carried a full goatee and was dressed in a long-sleeve white formal shirt tucked into dark brown long pants. Although he had some extra body fat on his belly, his shoulders and chest reflected that he'd been exercising recently. He stretched out his right hand, and James took it in a handshake.

"I am Oliver Ward," he said as they shook hands.

"Yes, sir. Please to meet you, sir." James replied.

"And this is my wife, Mrs. Ward," he said, turning to the right of him as he pushed his rectangular, gold frame spectacles off the bridge of his nose.

James turned slightly, and for the first time, he saw someone else in the room. She rose from the long, dark brown upholstered chair in the left corner of the room and approached him. Her hand was outstretched for a handshake, and James took it.

"Please to meet you, Mrs. Ward," he said, returning her firm handshake.

"It's my pleasure," she said, studying

his face through her black-rimmed glasses.

Mrs. Ward was dressed in a red and white skirt suit and, standing in heels, reached James' height. Braids and curls graced her hair and fitted well with her circular face.

"Sit, sit," Mr. Ward said, gesturing to the dark-stained, cherry, armless chairs in front of his desk.

James and Mrs. Ward sat in the chairs indicated while Mr. Ward returned to the chair behind his desk.

"Tell us about yourself, James," he said, leaning back in his chair.

"Well," James said, sitting rigidly in the chair, "I went to Sandy Lakes Secondary School and graduated with eight subjects."

"Yes, I saw that on your resume." Mr. Ward leaned forward and tapped the closed file in front of him on the desk.

James' smile briefly faltered as he wondered again if he would be fired before his probation period ended.

"What made you want to work at Glen's magazine?" Mrs. Ward asked.

He was asked this question during his interview, so he responded with the same answer.

The Wards nodded as they exchanged glances.

"And what are your plans for the future? What career path do you want to follow?" she asked him.

"I'd like to be a journalist," he replied immediately.

"A journalist," Mr. Ward said, leaning back in the chair, "in the printing or broadcasting field?"

"In the printing field," James replied as his smile returned.

"My dad was a journalist in the printing field," Mr. Ward said, "and he wanted me to become one too, and although I love the written word, I cannot put two words together to save my life."

James smiled, and Mrs. Ward laughed, her eyes twinkling as she fastened them on James.

"So," Mr. Ward continued, "when he realized that I had a business head and not a writing head, he decided to send me to get a degree in business."

James nodded.

"When it was our son's turn to choose his path," he continued, using a nod of his head to include Mrs. Ward, "to our surprise, he chose both."

"Wow," James said.

"Yes," Mrs. Ward said, "he has the head for both. They are like second nature to him."

"What about you, James?" Mr. Ward asked. "Who footsteps are you following?"

"Well, I think I'm following in my footsteps," James replied.

The Wards exchanged glances again, and the room fell silent as they stared at him.

James shifted uncomfortably in his chair, and Mr. Ward cleared his throat before leaning forward and asking, "When will you be pursuing your degree in journalism?"

Why are they asking me this? "I've decided to put it off for the next two years."

"Two years, I see. Why?" Mrs. Ward asked.

"Well, because I kept hearing that it is tough for university and college graduates to get a job in this field, and it is especially harder when they don't have any working experience. So, I've decided to get as many working experiences as possible before pursuing a degree, so that way–"

"When you graduate, you will also have a degree and working experience," Mrs. Ward said.

"Exactly," he exclaimed, swishing his right index finger.

"That's commendable, isn't it, Oliver?" Mrs. Ward looked over at her husband.

James tried to control his smile, but it spread from one ear to the next.

"Thank you," he said.

Mr. Ward nodded his agreement as he leaned back in his chair.

"Well, James," he said, "we are looking

for someone exactly like you!"

"Thank you, sir," he said, as his smile grew and the temperature in the room suddenly became warmer.

"Since purchasing this company," Mr. Ward continued, "we've been looking at ways to help individual young people looking at journalism as a career.

"Oh, okay," James said.

"So, we are looking into setting up an educational fund to help with this. Since we're only in the research stage right now, it involves going through resumes and talking with employees and applicants who we think we can help."

"And right now," Mrs. Ward said, "we can help you."

"Wait, what?" James smiled and laughed at the same time.

"Yes," Mrs. Ward said, "and that's why we're talking with you right now."

"Thank you!" he said, not knowing what else to say.

"You're welcome," they replied in unison.

"You may want to bring in your parents at our next meeting so we can go through the finer details and sign the contract," Mr. Ward suggested.

"My parents?" James asked, his eyes enlarging a little.

"Yes," he replied, "we know you are an adult, and you don't need your parents' permission to accept this offer, but it's not about that. It is a big decision, and it would be best to have someone to advise you as you move forward."

"Of course," James said, smiling sheepishly, "that would make sense, but do both of my parents have to be here?"

"No, no," Mr. Ward said, "one of them would be fine, but if both of them can come, it would be even better."

"Trust us on this, son," Mrs. Ward said, leaning forward and tapping him on the shoulder.

"Well, in that case, I'll bring my mom and uncle."

"Your uncle?" Mr. Ward asked as he and Mrs. Ward exchanged glances.

"Yes, sir, but he has been more like a father to me than an uncle."

"And your father, if you don't mind us asking, where is he?" Mrs. Ward asked, her eyes steady on his face.

"No, I don't mind you asking," he replied as his voice suddenly became hoarse. "Huh, by the time I was born, my father had already left my mom and me."

He cleared his throat. "Excuse me," he said.

"I'm sorry to hear that," Mr. Ward said.

"Thank you," James said, "but my uncle has been there for me. In truth, his entire family has been there for my mom and me."

Why am I telling them these things? Stop talking before they change their minds.

He bit down on his lower lip.

"Well, son, we will not keep you any longer," Mr. Ward said, standing and pushing back the chair with the back of his knees.

James jumped to his feet.

"We will get things settled on our end, and we will get back to you in a couple of days," he said, shaking James' hand.

"Yes, sir," James replied, and after thanking them again, he left the room, closing the door behind him.

"Wow," he mouthed before pumping his right fist.

He walked back to his office with a big smile on his face.

CHAPTER 9
THE SCHOLARSHIP

After returning to his office, the rest of the day went by in a blur for James, and when he walked through the front door of his home, he was humming. His mom was on the telephone.

"Okay, I'll call you back later, Thomas," she said as James removed his black leather laceless shoes by the door.

She was quiet for a few seconds before saying, "Okay, bye. Bye."

She returned the white cordless phone to its base on the black circular coffee table next to the brown upholstery chair she was sitting in.

"Hi, son," she greeted, smiling up at him.

"Hi, Mom," he returned and broke into a broad smile as he pulled off his grey socks.

"How was work?"

"Well," he said, walking towards her, "Mr. Ward called me into his office today."

"He did?" She held her breath. "Why?"

He kissed her on the forehead before dropping down next to her in the chair.

"Do you remember me telling you that the Wards mainly work from home? That they hardly show up at the office?" he asked.

"Yes," she said, nodding.

"Both Mr. and Mrs. Ward Sr. were there today."

His mom continued to hold her breath.

"When I got back from lunch, Mrs. Jones, the receptionist, told me that Mr. Ward wanted to see me in his office. So, I thought that maybe they were not pleased with my work and I was going to get fired or something else, but that wasn't the case," he replied, unable to keep the excitement from bubbling in his words.

She nodded again, searching his face for answers to questions she did not verbalize.

"It's quite the opposite. The Wards are..." James said.

His mom's right shoulder moved involuntarily, and her hand shook slightly.

"Mom, are you okay?"

The smile on his face disappeared as he stared down at her hand, which continued to shake.

"You are trembling!"

She quickly folded her arms across her chest.

"What... what," she said before she cleared her throat. "What did they say?"

"Mom," James said, "my news can wait. Are you sick? Are you coming down with something? What's going on?"

"I'm fine," she said, forcing a smile, "what did they talk to you about?"

"Okay, okay, I'll tell you," he said, but the smile did not return to his face. "They offered me a scholarship to attend the university and get my degree." His eyes were fixed on her arms before moving to her face.

She opened her mouth but closed it without saying anything. She opened it again and asked, "Why would they do that?"

"They want to help young people who want to work in journalism." A small smile tugged at the corner of his mouth.

"We don't need their money," she said, frowning, as she unfolded and refolded her arms.

"What... what do you mean?" James asked, a little taken aback by her words.

"We've made it this far by hard work, not by handouts."

"It's a scholarship, Mom, it's not charity, and even though we didn't get into everything, I'm sure that after I've gotten my degree, I'll have to work with them for several years or something as repayment."

She stood up, then, looking down at

him, said, "Say thank you, but no thank you, to them."

Then, turning her head, she headed for the kitchen.

"But Mom, this is an opportunity of a lifetime," James said, getting up and following her.

"I've told you this before, James. You can attend the university with the portion of the money I've already saved up for you, and I'll get the rest."

"I know, Mom, but you know there is more to it than me contributing to the tuition. You know it will be much easier for me to get the job I want later if I have some work experience, but with this scholarship, I wouldn't have to worry about anything."

"God will take care of that. You are a Christian. Where is your faith?" she asked as tears blurred her vision and rolled down her cheeks.

She stopped at the sink and turned on the tap.

"Mom, Mom, are you crying?" James asked after hearing the catch in her voice and the movement of her shoulders as she stood at the sink, gripping it.

She didn't reply but washed her hands before bending her head to wash her face in the empty sink.

"I thought this would make you happy.

I thought it was good news. It's not charity."

"We don't need Wards' money. You don't need their help," Janice replied, turning off the tap and reaching out for a tissue from the roll on a stand holder on the counter.

"It's not charity, Mom," James said pleadingly.

"You still don't need their help," She turned to look at him.

"Mom, please, what's wrong? I know there's more to this than just a scholarship. The only time I've ever seen you cry was when I was twelve, and I asked you about my father."

She abruptly turned away from him and steadied herself by grabbing the counter.

"Just do whatever you want," she said.

Then, stretching up her right arm, she opened the overhead cupboard and noisily took out two large white plates.

"Mom, please, you know me better than that. I'm not going to do whatever I want." James threw out his arms.

"Then please stop arguing with me about it and just don't accept the scholarship," she replied, walking over to the stove with the plates in her hands.

James sighed loudly. "I'm not arguing with you. It's just that I don't understand why you don't want me to accept it. I hear what you say about charity, but I still don't see where you're coming from."

His mom said nothing as she spooned white rice into a plate.

"Okay, okay," James said, rubbing his hairless chin. "I have a few days to think about it. Let's think about it some more, and maybe we'll see things differently by then."

"I'm not going to change my mind," she replied, putting down the plate with the rice and picking up the empty one.

"You might, or I might."

She did not reply.

James walked over to the sink and after washing and drying his hands, he kissed her on her forehead. The silence continued between them.

"How was your day, Mom?" he asked as he helped to set the table for their dinner.

She replied that it was fine, and they chit-chatted about how pleasant the weather was during the day.

James thanked God for their food before they ate, and they ate in silence for several minutes before his mother asked, "Stacy will only be away for two more months, right?

"Yes," he said, as a smile involuntarily creased the corners of his mouth, "and I can't wait to see her."

"That's good," she said, smiling.

"I hope she doesn't forget me by then," he said, a frown replacing his smile.

"She wouldn't forget you, son. She's in love with you and knows you're in love with her."
James blushed, and he tried to hide it by bending his head. His mom smiled.

"Mom?" he asked after a few seconds.

"Hum?" she answered with a mouthful of food.

"After Dad left us, did you ever fall in love with someone else?"

She involuntarily swallowed the food in her mouth and ended up coughing. She picked up the glass of water next to her plate and drank half of it.

"I wasn't expecting that question," she said, still coughing.

"Are you okay?"

"I'm fine, fine," she said, clearing her throat.

"Okay," he replied, "I know it's none of my business, but I've never seen you with anyone. Never. Why is that?"

The telephone rang, and she jumped out of the chair.

"Let me get that," she said, pushing away the chair with the back of her knees.

"But we don't usually answer the phone when eating."

"We usually don't, but sometimes we do."

"Mom," James said, throwing his hands

into the air.

"It might be important." She reached out for the receiver.

James shook his head, smiling, as he continued with his supper.

Even after eating, his mother was still on the telephone, and with him wanting to go to the library before going to Bible Studies at church, he quickly showered and left home with her still on the phone.

CHAPTER 10
I'M TELLING THE TRUTH

Janice waved goodbye to James just before he unlocked the front door, pulled it open, and disappeared behind it.

How much longer will this survey take?

She listened to him locking the door with his key.

The person on the other end continued questioning her, but it only lasted five more minutes. She rarely participated in telephone surveys. However, she did not expect James' question and wanted to avoid that conversation.

Although her appetite was no longer there, she sat and ate the rest of her supper. As she ate, her mind drifted to her past. She thought about the day she'd left the only home she'd ever known, and although it happened many years ago, it seemed like only yesterday.

Janice remembered driving down the dirt-paved road with Thomas. They were in his company's vehicle, and as they went, she looked through the tinted window and stared at the peeling whitewash bungalow that had been her home for the past sixteen years. Her heart felt like someone was slowly rolling a large stone across it, and as it rolled, it was slowly suffocating her.

As she sat quietly in the van for a few seconds, her thoughts, as though caught in a rabbit trap, pondered her mother's survival without her.

"It will be okay," Thomas said, as though reading her thoughts, "Mom will be okay, and so will you."

She nodded in response and, closing her eyes, slowly freed her heart from its trap.

"It wouldn't take us too long to get there," Thomas said after a few minutes of silence.

She nodded, and a few tears slipped down her cheeks.

They drove silently for a while, and every new vehicle they encountered pushed Janice's sadness aside and replaced it with curiosity.

"How far away from here do you and Amanda live?" she asked him.

"It's about forty-five minutes, give or take, by car."

She nodded and asked him the name of their area, and he told her.

"I've heard of it, but I've never been in

that area before," she replied.

"Don't worry. It's a good place to raise a family. You'll like it."

They continued talking until Thomas brought the vehicle to a stop before a grey-painted chain-linked fence.

"We're here," he announced, smiling broadly.

Janice slowly opened the door and jumped out of the van. She stood looking at the house for a few seconds. A grey chain-link fence and trimmed grass surrounded the brown and white wall bungalow. Thomas took out two black plastic bags, and Janice grabbed the last one. He lifted the V-shaped latch at the top of the gate, and they walked into the yard. Janice looked up in time to see the white-painted door flying open, and the face she'd seen in the photograph only the day before appeared at the door.

Amanda's cheeks were now fatter than in the photo, and the blue and white floral dress she wore fitted well around her pregnant tummy.

"Come in, come in," she said, motioning with her hand and stepping back inside as they walked to the top of the four narrow concrete steps that lead to the inside of the house.

"You can put the bag there," Amanda said, indicating a spot with her hand.

Janice entered the house and put the bag on the white tiled floor in the area that Amanda pointed out.

"Come here," Amanda said, opening her arms.

Janice, slightly taller than her, walked into her open arms.

"I am so happy to finally meet you," Amanda said as she hugged her.

"I'm pleased to meet you too," Janice replied.

"Hi, Honey," Thomas said as he placed the two bags next to the one Janice had put down.

"Hi, Sweetheart," Amanda replied as she and Janice separated.

Thomas and Amanda briefly kissed.

"Okay, guys," Thomas said, exhaling heavily, "I have to go back to work, but before I do, let me grab a 7-Up from the fridge and leave you two to get acquainted."

"Okay, Sweetheart," Amanda said as he walked towards the kitchen. Then, turning back to look at Janice, she asked, "How are you?"

"Me? I'm fine, thank you," Janice replied, looking around the house.

They were standing in the living room. It had two extended upholstery beige chairs and a light brown single sitter arranged around a black oval table with a transparent vase with red artificial flowers. Two photos of Thomas and Amanda were framed and hanging on the wall. A picture of flowers and another one of a bird's image in an apple tree were also there. There was a black T.V. on a dark brown stand with several ornaments on it.

"You have a lovely home," Janice said.

"Thanks," Amanda replied, smiling.

Thomas returned to the living room with a green can of 7-Up glued to his lips.

"Ahh..." he said after he removed the can from his lips. "I'm off."

He kissed Amanda, then turning to Janice, he rested a hand on her shoulder and said, "Everything will be fine."

She nodded, and a few seconds later, he walked through the door. He closed and locked it behind him.

"Come," Amanda said, taking her by the hand, "let me show you your room, and then we can put your things in it."

"Okay," Janice replied, walking with her.

They passed the kitchen on the right and the dining room on their left. Then, a few steps down, they reached a room on their left with a washroom opposite it.

"This is your room," Amanda said, leading them through the opened door.

A light shade of pink paint was on the

walls in the bedroom. Janice initially mistook the colour for white. She also observed that the room was larger than the one she had with her mom. A square window had a thin pink polka-dot curtain covering it. A neatly made-up, double-size bed was in the middle of the room, and a white-painted pine wardrobe was next to the door. A small bookshelf was also there, and two paintings of flowers were also on the walls.

"Is this for me?" she asked, staring around the room.

"Yes," Amanda replied, "but if you don't like the colours, don't worry, we …."

Janice hugged her, and she stopped talking.

"This is so beautiful, thank you."

"Oh," Amanda replied, surprised, "you're welcome." When they parted, Amanda said, "Come, let's go get your things, but let's eat something first. Are you hungry?"

"Yes, I am," Janice replied, bending her head slightly. "I feel as if I can eat two full plates of food right now."

Amanda laughed, and they headed for the kitchen.

As they ate, they talked, and Janice found out that Amanda's mom had spent three weeks with them and had left only three days before Janice came. She was staying in the room that was now Janice's. As Thomas said, they were not planning on Janice coming to live with them so soon, but they were sure that God would help them with this change in the plan.

Amanda's mom wanted to visit them after the baby was born, but she had an appointment for knee surgery around the birth time. Nevertheless, she would visit again as soon as she was back on her feet.

The rest of the day and Sunday with Thomas and Amanda flew by quickly as Janice settled into her new environment. Thomas drove her to school whenever he had the company's vehicle, but she took the bus the rest of the time.

On the following Saturday morning arrived, around eleven o'clock, Janice sat in the front seat with Thomas at the wheel of his company's vehicle. She was dressed in long black maternity pants and a white t-shirt with writings on its back. Thomas and Amanda had purchased the pants and a few more maternity clothes for her, although her baby bump was barely visible.

They drove down a long concrete driveway that formed a Y and brought the van to a stop at the front of a massively elegant concrete house. Several long glass windows with drawn curtains surrounded the front of the house. Janice and Thomas stepped out of the van. They surveyed the beauty of their surroundings as they walked closer to and up the steps. The siblings exchanged glances as Thomas pressed the white doorbell.

A few minutes later, the large brown-stained wooden door was pulled open, and a tall, light-brown skin, middle-aged man dressed in a formal white shirt and black pants stood there.

"Good morning. How may I help you?" he asked.

"Good morning," Thomas said, "I am Thomas Shepherd, and this is my sister, Janice. We are here to see the Wards. They're expecting us."

"Yes, come in," he said, stepping aside to allow them to enter the house.

Janice's mouth fell open after entering the house. They stood on a wooden, elevated, brown-stained island, and Janice stared around the house.

"Come this way, please," the man said as he quickly led them through the house.

Janice's mouth remained open as she walked down the three-step island. The steps went all around the elevated entrance. They walked across a large decorated black and white rectangular carpet lying on white tiles and a black and white wooden and wrought iron staircase with the bottom of the steps spread out like a wedding dress. The stairway led to a balcony. A large black piano with a white bench was next to the stairs. Beautiful photos lined the wall. There were also long and thick, black and white pillars that looked as though made to be precisely where they were. They magnified the already elegant house.

Their guide brought them to the front of a dark brown wooden door, and after knocking twice on it, a male voice called out, "Come!"

He turned the knob, pushed the door open and entered the room. They followed him in.

"Thomas Shepherd and his sister Janice Shepherd are here to see you, Mr. and Mrs. Ward," he announced.

The room was a home office, and Janice was surprised to find it not decorated in black and white. Most of the large furnishings were wooden and stained in light and dark brown. The office had long rectangular glass windows, and with the cream, see-through curtains drawn, the morning light from outside flooded the room, and with the windows opened, a cooling breeze also filled the room.

Mr. Ward sat in a brown high-back office chair behind a medium-sized mahogany rectangular desk. Two cream and gold table lamps were on both sides of the table, and a large wooden and golden ship, which looked like Noah's ark, was on the right side of the desk. A family photo, a dark blue pen in a wooden pen holder and folders were also on the desk.

Mrs. Ward was sitting in one of the two brown chairs in front of the desk. Bookshelves filled with books were on both sides of the room, and Janice felt the urge to walk over to one of them, reach out for a book, and sit and read it. Instead, she pulled her eyes away from them by looking down at a long, black leather chair next to a bookshelf on the left side of the room.

Mr. Ward came out from behind the desk and shook their hands, and Mrs. Ward stood and did the same before thanking the man, George, for bringing them into the room. George nodded and, turning around, left the room and closed the door behind him. Mr. Ward offered Janice and Thomas seats in the leather chair beside the bookshelf. They took them.

Janice stared at Mrs. Ward and thought she was even more beautiful in person than in the newspaper.

Mrs. Ward was a short woman with long black hair that ended in curls at the nape of her neck. She was dressed in a red skirt suit with the skirt covering her knees. She was also wearing a skin-tone stocking and red high-heeled shoes. Mrs. Ward adjusted the chair at the desk to face them when they sat in the leather chair.

Mr. Ward had a headful of grey and black hair and was dressed in a black and blue suit. He also returned to his seat behind the desk.

"How can we help you?" Mrs. Ward asked, making eye contact with Janice.

Janice opened her mouth to speak, but her lips trembled instead.

What's wrong with me? I thought I was prepared for this.

She tried to speak again, but the trembling continued, and suddenly, water rushed into her eyes, and she speedily blinked them away. Thomas reached out and squeezed her hand.

"My sister is pregnant with your son's baby," he stated, looking from Mr. to Mrs. Ward.

"Oh, I see," Mr. Ward said and then cleared his throat.

"What are you looking for from us?" Mrs. Ward questioned.

"My sister is not going to abort the baby. She is going to give them up for adoption."

"I see," Mrs. Ward said as she and her husband exchanged glances.

"Since the child is your grandchild," he continued, "she thought that you could help to get the child into a good home."

"I see," Mr. Ward said, leaning back in his chair and causing it to rock slightly.

"How old are you, dear?" Mrs. Ward asked, looking at Janice.

Janice bowed her head and bit down on her lower lip while Thomas spoke. Now, she lifted her head to Mrs. Ward but avoided meeting the older woman's eyes. She slowly parted her lips as she willed them not to tremble and pleaded with her tears to stay away.

She closed her mouth, cleared her throat, and answered, "I'm sixteen."

"And where and when did you and my son meet?" she asked.

Janice's eyes darted to Thomas, and he squeezed her hand again.

"I think that's a question for your son," Thomas replied.

"Do my son know that you are pregnant?" Mr. Ward asked.

"No," Janice whispered.

"Well, don't you think it would be best to talk with him first? After all, the two of you are in a relationship, aren't you?" Mrs. Ward asked.

"I didn't say we were in a relationship." Suddenly, Janice's shoulders stiffened. She did not like Mrs. Ward's tone of voice. She met Mrs. Ward's eyes.

Things are not supposed to go this way.

Thomas and Amanda tried to talk me out of this, but I wouldn't listen. I insisted that this was the best way because Mrs. Ward is known for her charitable work at the only orphanage on the island.

"Then the two of you have broken up?" Mr. Ward asked as he leaned forward in the chair.

"We were never in a relationship." An unwelcome shiver ran through her body.

"I see," Mrs. Ward said, crossing her legs, "so it was a one-time thing?"

"Yes. No," Janice said.

"Look," Mrs. Ward said, "let's cut to the chase. You are not the first group who tried to shake us down for money."

"Although," Mr. Ward added, "the two of you are the first to propose adoption for our supposed grandchild."

"You think that I'm lying? I'm not. I'm telling you the truth. The baby is his."
Mrs. Ward shook her head as she stood.

"As long as I live, I will never understand people like you," she said, looking from Thomas to Janice.

"People like us?" Janice asked as her upper body jumped backwards as though shoved in the chest.

"Yes, people like you, people who go around trying to enrich their lives by destroying other people's lives," was Mrs. Ward's quick response.

Before she knew it, Janice jumped out of the chair, and Thomas stood next to her.

"The only person doing the destroying here is your son," she said, her voice rising as she looked at them.

Mr. Ward rose from his seat.

Janice bit down on her lower lip and briefly closed her eyes.

"He raped me! Your son raped me!" Janice said through clenched teeth

The room suddenly fell silent, and Mrs. Ward jumped as though slapped in the face. Then, slowly, her lips curved into a smile, and slowly, the room filled with a deep chuckle, which developed into laughter. Janice and Thomas exchanged glances, and as suddenly as the laughter began, it stopped.

"So, let us get this straight," she said, looking at Mr. Ward, whose arms were folded across his chest, "at first you said that it was not a one-time thing, and now you're saying it was rape?"

"It was always rape," Janice retorted.

"Then where are the police? Where is the police report?" Mrs. Ward asked.

"He raped me," Janice said as she looked from Mrs. to Mr. Ward.

"Look, this has gone on long enough," Mr. Ward said, "I want the two of you to leave my house and, for your own sake, stop spreading lies about my son and keep away from my family!"

"I'm telling you the truth. I'm not lying," Janice said, her voice rising.

"If you don't," Mr. Ward continued as though Janice had not spoken, "and if I hear a word about this from anywhere, by the time we are finished with you, both of you will be begging for me to give you the crumbs from my table."

"Please," Janice pleaded, wringing her hands, "I am telling you the truth. I am not lying."

"Get out of my house before I call the cops and have you arrested for trespassing," Mrs. Ward said as anger burned in her eyes, but it did not reach her voice.

Janice did not move.

"Get out," she stated calmly. "You cannot come into our home and accuse our son of assaulting you and getting you pregnant and then turn around and ask us to help you with the child? Are you crazy or something?"

"I'm..." Janice began.

"Get out!" Mrs. Ward said, almost shouting now as she pointed to the door.

"Let's go, Jan," Thomas whispered, leading her by the shoulders towards the door.

Wordlessly, she allowed him to lead her, and to her surprise, when Thomas opened the door, George, the man who had brought them into the room, was standing there with his right hand in the air as if he was about to knock on the door.

I wonder how long he was standing there. Did he hear our conversation? Janice thought.

"Come this way, please," he stated.

They retraced their steps to the outside of the house, and when they got to the vehicle, they silently entered it. They drove down the driveway with tears soundlessly rolling down Janice's cheeks.

"What's wrong with me, Teddy Bear? What's wrong with me? You and Amanda told me this was not a good idea, but I didn't listen."

"It's okay, Jan, it's okay, you're just a child, but I'm the adult, and I should have just said no and left it at that," Thomas took his eyes off the road for a few seconds.

"No, no," Janice said, "if you had said no, I would have just done it on my own because I was certain that my plan would work. What was I thinking?"

A motorbike with a loud exhaust pulled up alongside the jeep as they stopped at a red light.

"I wasn't going to tell them about the attack, but they made me so angry, and before I knew it, the words were out." Janice continued.

"I know and understand, but it is for the best. Everything will be okay."

"I should have lied and said that I was pregnant with my boyfriend's baby and needed them to help me with the adoption. Things probably would have gone a lot better."

Janice blew her nose into the white tissue she pulled from a square grey box in the cubby between her and Thomas.

"Jan–" Thomas said.

"Yeah, I know, you wouldn't have approved of being a part of a lie."

Thomas nodded.

They drove silently for a few minutes before Thomas brought the vehicle to a stop at a curb in the road. He parked the jeep and turned to look at her.

"Jan," he said, "have you thought about keeping the baby?"

"What?" Janice stared at him.

"Amanda and I are more than willing to help you. This baby and our child can grow up together."

"What?"

"Jan, what happened to you is horrible, and I am so sorry. It is amazing, though, that you have decided to bring the pregnancy to full term, too."

She nodded.

"Then keep the child. Amanda and I will help you to take care of them. This baby can grow up with our child," he said.

"I don't know about this," Janice said, finally finding her voice, "I'm only sixteen. I'm just a child, too. I can't be a mother to this baby."

"I understand, trust me, I do," Thomas said, exhaling slowly, "but Amanda and I will be here to help you."

"I don't know about this, Teddy," Janice said as she shook her head. "I can't be a mother and go to school at the same time. It would be too much for me, and besides, I will never be able to love this baby, and that will be far worse than giving them up for adoption."

"I understand, but you don't have to decide now. Just think about it for a little while, and in the meantime, we will look more into the adoption process."

"Okay," Janice said quietly and suddenly, like a deflated balloon, she slumped in the seat and exhaled slowly. She turned away from looking at him and gazed through the window beside her.

They were parked next to a field where three brown and white cows were grazing.

Thomas started the engine, and as they pulled away from the curb, Janice began biting her short, unpainted fingernails.

CHAPTER 11
FATHER

By the following morning, James already decided he would not accept the scholarship from the Wards. So, as he sat to eat breakfast with his mom, he told her of his decision.

"Your uncle and aunt will be having dinner with us tonight. I'd like to talk to you about something, and it will be easier for me to do so with them here."

"Is it your health?" James immediately asked.

"We will talk about it later, but in the meantime, hold off on giving your workplace an answer about the scholarship."

"I don't see why I should wait." James slowly chewed on the oats in his mouth as he searched her face for some answers. "It's best to just get it over with."

She smiled at him. "I know, son. I know that you don't like to put things off."

He returned her smile.

"Just hold off until tonight," she said.

"Does this mean that you've changed your mind about me accepting the scholarship?"

"Tonight."

"Okay, Mom, okay," James said, raising one hand.

She nodded before saying, "Eat up now. You don't want to miss your bus."

"No, I don't," James said sulkily.

So, they ate, and before long, James was sitting in a blue and red public bus that would take him to work. A boy captured his attention, and James judged him to be about ten years old. The boy was playing with his handheld game.

The boy was dressed in a school uniform of a cream short-sleeved shirt and brown shorts. He was sitting next to a man James judged to be his father because they both shared the same protruding forehead and slightly protruding nose. The man was reading a newspaper. The boy looked up from his game and tapped his father on the shoulder. His father leaned his ears close to his mouth, and he whispered something to him. His father chuckled, and the boy smiled before returning to his handheld game. Then, for countless times, James thought about his father and silently asked, "Where are you?"

His thoughts drifted to when he didn't like looking at the televised Evening News, but his mom did. So, she offered to add one dollar to his weekly allowance for every day he looked at the evening news.

One evening, when he was in his twelfth year, his mom, uncle, aunt and cousin, Sammy, were sitting in front of the television set. They were looking at the local evening news. As they watched, the broadcaster talked about a five-year-old girl born with a rare genetic disorder called Diamond Blackfan Anemia. It meant that her bone marrow was not producing enough red blood cells; to complicate it even more, she had a rare blood type.

The doctors told her parents that the best treatment for her was a blood transfusion every three to six weeks until she could undergo a bone marrow transplant. However, the clinic had a limited supply of her required B- blood type. Therefore, her dad, whose blood type was the same as hers, gave her his blood for over two years. After this, her parents campaigned, asking others to donate blood, and many people did. Then, shortly afterwards, the girl underwent a bone marrow transplant, and she responded well to it. With the transplant, her bone marrow was starting to produce enough red blood cells. Therefore, she did not need any more blood transfusions.

As James watched and listened to the girl's story, he wondered about his father, and when the news was over, he went to bed in the bedroom that he shared with his cousin Sammy. As usual, his mom entered the room to bid them goodnight, and after she sat at the edge of his bed, he said, "Mom."

"Mm," she replied, looking down at him and touching his face as she smiled.

"Who is my father?"

The smile on her face immediately dropped, and her lips parted as though she was about to speak, but instead, they began to tremble, and tears rushed to her eyes, but she turned her face away from him. James scrambled from under his covers and threw his arms around her neck.

"I'm sorry, Mom, I'm sorry. I shouldn't have asked you about him. I wouldn't ask you about him again, I promise. Please don't cry."

Then the tears came, and her shoulders shook as James and Sammy heard her cry.

"Aunty, Aunty!" James cried.

"Mom, Mom!" Sammy called.

His aunt and uncle rushed into the room.

"I didn't mean to make her cry," James said immediately.

He frowned, and both hands landed on the top of his head before dropping lifelessly at his sides on the bed.

"What happened?" his uncle asked.

"I don't know," James said, removing his arms from his mom and getting out of bed.

"I just asked her about my dad and...." James said, his voice trailing off.

"It's okay, guys," Aunty Amanda said. "It's okay."

His aunt placed her hands on Janice's shoulders and, bending close to her right ear, said, "Janice, let's go to your bedroom and let the boys get some rest."

Janice nodded, got up from the bed, and walked out of the room with Amanda's arms around her waist.

After their parents left, the cousins lay silently in the semi-dark bedroom. Light from a nearby streetlamp kept their cream-painted room from engulfing into total darkness. A writing desk made from pine wood separated the boys' double-sized beds.

"Sammy, are you still awake?" James whispered.

"Maybe."

"Do you think the reason why my mom is always sad is because of my dad?"

"She's not always sad," Sammy replied, propping his head up with his hand as he looked over at him. "She's sad most of the time, but not always."

"But do you think it's because of my dad?" James turned his head in his cousin's direction.

"Maybe... I guess," Sammy said, shrugging slightly.

James was silent for a few seconds before he said, "If I ever get married, I will never leave my family." His jawline hardened as he spoke.

"Yeah, me too." Sammy dropped his head onto the pillow.

The young cousins were silent for a few seconds, and all they could hear was the ticking of the black and blue Batman clock on the wall next to the door.

"Aunty Janice will be okay," Sammy said as a yawn escaped him.

James didn't reply but closed his eyes, and before long, they drifted off to sleep.

James was jolted to the present when the bus rocked side to side, climbing in and out of potholes. He glanced over at the father and son before stretching his hand and pressing the buzzer for the upcoming bus stop. As usual, he arrived at work on time and buried himself in the folders on his desk.

"Are you skipping lunch today?" Simon asked from the other side of the desk.

James looked up at him as his fingers continued to move across the keyboard.

"Hum?"

"Lunch, food, eat. It's noon." Simon tapped the silver colour watch on his left hand.

James stopped typing and lifted the left cuff on his white shirt to look at the black leather watch there.

"Already?" James looked down at the watch. "I didn't realize it was so late. Thanks, Simon. See you in an hour."

He signed out of the computer system. He pulled out his black backpack from under the table and, standing, struggled it onto his back. He then headed for the door. He pulled the door open, stepped into the hallway, and immediately collided with someone dressed in a black suit.

"Sorry," James said, stepping out of the man's path.

"No, no. It's my fault. I'm sorry. I wasn't looking where I was going," the man replied.

James looked up to see who the person was.

"Hi, I'm Matthew Ward." The man stretched his hand.

"I'm James, Mr. Ward," he replied, taking his hand, and two vigorous handshake ensued. Mr. Ward studied his face briefly, and with his head slightly tilted to the left, he asked, "Have we met before?"

"No sir," James replied as the handshake ended.

"Excuse me, Mr. Ward," a man James recognized as a writer at the magazine said,

"Can I have a word with you?"

"Yes, sure, I was coming to see you." Then, returning his attention to James, he said, "Excuse me, James."

"Yes, sure." James stepped aside.

James stood looking at Matthew Ward's back for a few seconds before turning and leaving the building for his lunch break.

The remainder of the day sped by, and as James made his way home that evening, his heart kept beating faster than usual, and he pleaded with God to calm him. He was afraid of losing his mom.

So, after stopping off at the usual bus stop, James hurried home and, using his keys, entered the home. Immediately, his nose was bombarded with baked chicken, macaroni pie, apple pie and other foods. They waltzed their way into his nostrils, and his belly growled, and his fears fell from him like a waterfall.

"I'm home," he announced over the laughter from the kitchen.

"There he is," Uncle Thomas cried, walking out of the kitchen and hugging him before he could take off his shoes.

His uncle was about an inch shorter than him, wearing blue jeans and a light blue formal shirt tucked into his jeans. His curly hair was cut low, and he had recently trimmed his extended goatee.

"Hi, uncle," he greeted, returning his hug.

"My turn," Aunty Amanda said as she walked out of the kitchen and hugged him.

His aunt, dressed in blue jeans and a dark grey short-sleeved cotton top over her pants, had grown into a plump woman. Her dry curls hairstyle was combed into a bun.

"Hi, son," his mom called from the kitchen.

"Hi, Mom," he called back before bending and removing his shoes. He then asked while turning to his aunt and uncle after stepping out of his shoes, "How is Sammy?"

"He's good," she replied, "in fact, he called yesterday and had some good news. He said that two days before, when he and two other missionaries were sharing tracks and talking with some local people, they led a family of three to the Lord Jesus Christ."

"Praise the Lord," James said, smiling involuntarily.

"Indeed," Uncle Thomas said.

"Sometimes I wonder if I'd misunderstood the Lord's will for me about going on this trip with Sammy," James said as he slipped out his socks.

"You're right where the Lord wants you to be, honey," his aunt said.

His mom emerged from the kitchen with a familiar pink and white floral platter filled with baked chicken.

"Hi, Mom. I see we're in for a real feast tonight."

"You see, right," she replied, smiling over her shoulder as she put the platter on the dining table.

"Let me help set the table," Aunty Amanda said, turning to the kitchen.

"Right behind you, Dear," Uncle Thomas said.

"Dinner will be ready soon, son. In the meantime, you can wash up."

"Okay, Mom," James said, kissing her on the forehead before she returned to the kitchen, and he went to the washroom.

In addition to the baked chicken, macaroni pie, and apple pie, there were rice, peas, green vegetable salad, potato salad, and soft drinks. As they ate, the Shepherds talked and laughed, and after dinner, they put the dishes away and went to sit in the U-shaped living room. The light-brown upholstery living room suite encircled an oval-shaped, glass-top coffee table. A crystal-looking vase with artificial light-brown flowers was at the center of the table. The table was on a floral, dark brown, rectangular mat.

On both sides of the long chair in the room stood bamboo floor lamps, and family and store-brought photos decorated the walls.

James and his mom sat in the long chair facing the light brown television set on a stand. A VCR and ornaments were also on the TV stand. Thomas and Amanda sat on the loveseat next to them, and they continued to chat and laugh until the room grew silent.

Uncle Thomas cleared his throat and broke the silence among them.

"If you don't mind, Jan," he said, "I would like us to begin with a word of prayer."

She nodded, and when Thomas finished praying, everyone said, Amen.

"James," his mom said, turning her entire body to face him, "I love you very much, son, and I don't want you ever to doubt that. Okay?"

"Okay," James said, nodding and swallowing hard as he thought, *Here it comes.*

"This is about your father," she told him.

"My... my father?"

I never thought, not in a zillion years, that those words would ever come out of her mouth.

"I know you think he'd abandoned us, and I've never done anything to correct that thought. However, that's not what happened," his mom continued, looking down at her interlocked hands.

"It isn't?" he asked, his eyes enlarging.

She took a deep, slow breath, and after slowly letting it out, she said, "Son, I became pregnant with you through an assault."

James frowned, then stopped. He frowned again.

"Wait, what?"

His mother rubbed her forehead.

"Wait, attacked? What do you mean by *attack*?"

"One night, when I was alone at home, someone broke into the house and overpowered me," she said, rubbing her forehead.

James' eyes darted to his uncle and aunt, searching their faces for clarity about his mother's words, but he found none. His eyes then zipped back to her.

"You mean..., I was conceived when someone assaulted you? You mean I'm a child of assault?" His voice rose and fell.

His mother nodded, reaching out for his hand, but he pulled it out of her reach.

"I don't understand what you're saying to me," he said.

"You do understand, son, you do. You just need to take a deep breath and slowly let it out. I still have more to say to you."

He saw the flicker of pain in her eyes and refused to acknowledge it by looking over her shoulder.

"It can't be any worse than this," he said, throwing his hands into the air and shaking his head.

"The person who attacked me...my attacker is Matthew Ward."

Matthew Ward, Matthew Ward, Matthew Ward, who is he, and why does this name sound familiar? James thought, searching his mind for the connection, but he couldn't find it.

He shook his head to clear his mind.

"Is he still in jail?" he asked, looking from his mother to his uncle and aunt.

"No," his mom said bitterly, "I never pressed charges against him."

She swallowed hard.

"My attacker is Oliver Ward's son. You're working for them at Glen's Magazine."

"My... my..."

James jumped up from the chair and bolted for the washroom. He made it there just in time, and the white toilet bolt readily accepted his sickness.

Janice immediately got up to follow him, but her brother stopped her by saying, "Give him a few minutes."

He waved his hand, indicating that she should sit down again.

James returned to a quiet living room several minutes later and sat in his vacated seat.

"I guess feeding you so much food before this conversation was not such a good idea," his mother said.

James smiled slightly.

"I don't understand any of this," James said, scratching his head before his hands fell lifelessly to his sides.

"You will, son. You will," his mom said, reaching out for his hand.

He did not pull it away this time, and she squeezed it for a few seconds before letting go. Her hands trembled, and she took a deep breath, trying to stop the trembling from overtaking her entire body. She slowly slipped her hand under her legs, and they stopped trembling. She looked over at her brother and sister-in-law.

"I have so many questions, Mom, but I don't want to upset you by asking them."

"I'm going to tell you what happened," she said, "and if you have any questions after that, I'm willing to answer them."

"Okay." James nodded. "But are you sure?"

"Yes, I'm sure. I'll be fine."

He nodded.

"The night I was attacked, I was in my bedroom just chilling out, as you young people say, and listening to music, and the next thing I knew, someone was standing in my room. I tried to fight him off, but it was no use." Her head was slowly filling with pressure, but after taking a few deep breaths, the tension in her head eased. She continued. "My attacker thought I had hired him to do this horrible thing to me. I tried to tell him I didn't hire him, but it was too late by the time he finally believed me." Her hands started to tremble again, and she pressed her legs down on them.

"I saw his face just before he left," she stated. She swallowed quietly. "At first, I thought I did a face transplant on him because I'd seen his face in the newspapers recently, but after seeing his photo in the papers the following day, there was no doubt that it was him. It was him."

The room fell silent as his mom's gaze fixed on something only she saw. Then, after a few minutes, she sniffled and took a deep breath before continuing.

"When ... when the doctor said that I was pregnant, adoption seemed to be the only choice, so I went to his parents for help. Your uncle Thomas was with me, but that meeting didn't go well."

Uncle Thomas nodded, and his mom smiled absentmindedly.

"What happened?"

"They didn't believe me. The Wards simply didn't believe me," Janice said, raising and dropping her shoulders as she sniffled again.

"Wait," James said, "since you were going to give me up for adoption, how come I am here with you? Did they somehow prevent me from getting adopted? Why would they do that?"

James saw his uncle and aunt move slightly through his peripheral vision. However, they remained silent.

"No, not exactly," his mom replied as she tried to push down the memories that threatened to consume her mind.

"Then what? How did you end up raising me?"

His voice broke on a few words.

"Oh, son." She pulled her hands from under her legs and reached for his hand as she inched closer. "On our way home from meeting with the Wards, your uncle asked me to consider keeping you instead of giving you up for adoption."

For a brief moment, her mind travelled back to the day she was in her new home with her brother and sister-in-law. She was sitting in the living room, and Amanda, who was in her bedroom, called out, "He's moving! He's moving, Janice! Come quickly."

Janice rushed into the room and found Amanda, dressed in a red and white floral maternity dress, lying on the bed with her hand on her belly and her plump face glowing.

"Give me your hand," she said, tentatively reaching for it.

Hesitantly, Janice allowed her to take her hand and guided it to her belly. As soon as her hand touched Amanda's stomach, something hit it, and she jumped back, pulling her hand away. Then, a huge smile burst across her face.

"Can I do it again?" she asked.

Amanda grinned and once again took her hand and gently laid it on her tummy, and this time, instead of hitting her hand, the baby gently touched it. At least, that's how it felt to her. Janice removed her hand and sat next to Amanda.

"Is this what's going to happen with me, too?" she asked.

"Yes," Amanda said.

"But I'm only sixteen. I don't know anything about being a mother."

"I know, sweetheart, but I don't know anything about being a mother either, but your brother and I will help each other, and we will help you. You will not be alone."

"I'm scared; besides, my life is already over." Janice chewed her lower lip.

"Your life is not over, and although this is not the ideal situation, you have a life growing inside you. You are about to bring another life into this world, and with God's help, you will be able to handle everything," Amanda replied as she squeezed her hand.

"But what will happen when I do not

love the baby? I don't think I can love this baby," Janice said quietly.

James's voice slowly pulled her away from the past and back to the present.

"What was that, son?" she asked after meeting his expectant eyes.

"How could you keep me, let alone love me?" Anguish finally broke through his voice, giving it a high-pitchiness that was not usually there.

She was silent for a few seconds as tears gathered in her eyes.

"I grew to love you as you grew inside of me," she replied as tears silently ran down her cheeks. She wiped them away with the palm of her hand.

"But how could you love me? Why do you love me? Every time you look at me, don't I remind you of that horrible night?" His face was distorted as though he was someone in physical pain.

Then, as though suddenly hit by a lightning bolt, he involuntarily jumped in his seat, and a blank stare followed. Then the look of someone who was just relieved from constipation replaced it.

"I now understand why you are always so sad. It's because of me. I am the reason why you are always sad! You should have just given me up for adoption or left me at a church or something. That would have been better than a life of sadness for you."

She opened her mouth to reply, but James said, "Please don't say any more, Mom, please don't."

"What kind of person am I? Who am I?" he whimpered like a wounded animal.

He stood, and without looking at anyone, he walked out of the room and entered his bedroom. Janice and Thomas rose to follow him, and Thomas said, "Let me go and talk to him, Jan."

Janice hesitated slightly before nodding and sitting down again. Thomas left the room.

"Everything will be alright," Amanda said to her, "Everything will be alright."

Janice chewed her lower lip and then, releasing it, asked, "Did I make the right choice? Should I have just listened to my mother and aborted him?"

After a few seconds of staring at her, Amanda replied, "You know the answer to those questions already. You are just scared because of James' pain, but he will be fine, and so will you."

"But did you see his face? He looked like his entire world was just destroyed. He doesn't deserve this. He didn't ask for this," Janice said, her voice breaking.
"Give him some time. He will pull through. He has you, us, and above all, Jesus."

"Jesus? I can't think about Jesus right

now," Janice said, shaking her head.

"Why not? He loves you, Janice, and although you know about Him and try to live the Christian life, you keep putting off getting saved. You're hurting so much, Honey, and He's the only one who can heal you. Please, Jan."

"I can't, Amanda. I still can't think about being saved yet," she said, sinking back into the upholstered chair and closing her eyes.

"What are you waiting for? You have been saying this for the past twenty years."

"Stop worrying about me." She covered her face with her hands. "I'm thirty-five years old now, not sixteen, and if I can't take care of myself by now, well..."

"Oh, Sweetie...," Amanda said before allowing her voice to drop.

Silence filled the room, and although Amanda was eager to break it and desperately wanted to comfort her sister-in-law with a hug, she did not move or say anything to her. Instead, she silently prayed.

CHAPTER 12
IN TROUBLE

Thirty-six-year-old Matthew Ward was drinking brandy in his parents' home library when the door was pushed open, and his father walked in.

"Are you okay, son?" he asked after seeing the shot glass in his hand.

"Yeah, sure," Matthew replied, raising and dropping his hand in greeting after sipping his drink.

His father walked behind the desk and sat in the high-back black leather chair.

"Dad?" Matthew glanced over at him.

"Hmm?" his father replied without looking up from the white sheet of paper he'd picked up from his desk.

"I met both copy typists today and collided into one of them, but no one got hurt."

"Good, good," his father replied, lifting his head and looking at him over the rim of his glasses.

"What do we know about the Shepherd boy? I think his first name is John, no, James, yes, James?" Matthew looked at him over his almost empty glass.

"Why do you want to know about him?" his father asked sharply.

"I don't know. It's just that since running into James, something about him keeps gnawing at me. I could have sworn we met before." He emptied the last of the brandy in his mouth.

"Maybe you've seen him near the office."

"Maybe," Matthew replied, briefly losing track of everything around him.

A soft knock came on the door before it was slowly pushed open.

"I'm turning in for the night," a slender brown-skinned woman said upon entering the room.

"Okay, Honey," Matthew replied, "I'll join you there shortly."

"Okay," she replied, smiling at him.

She looked at her father-in-law and said, "Goodnight, Dad."

"Goodnight, Tracy," he replied.

She turned and walked through the door.

"How is the adoption process coming along?" Mr. Ward asked as the door closed.

"It's coming along. We have an appointment with the adoption agency next week," Matthew replied, exhaling heavily.

"How many have you visited so far, ten,

eleven?"

Matthew laughed softly. "Just two, Dad, and don't give up on us so quickly and don't worry about it either. The title 'Ward' will not die with me."

His dad stared at him briefly before saying, "I need to talk with you tomorrow before you go into the office."

"Okay," Matthew said, yawning, "and I better turn in for the night."

"Okay, son, goodnight."

"Goodnight, Dad," Matthew said, putting his glass on a silver tray. Two other glasses and a bottle of half-empty Baileys were on the tray.

Matthew left the room, closing the door behind him. His father continued to sit at the desk, and after the door was closed, he unlocked the drawer under the desk and took out a light brown envelope. He examined it for a few seconds before exhaling loudly.

The following morning, Matthew whistled when he walked through the home office door. He was dressed in long, black dress pants with a solid white long-sleeve shirt.

"Hi, Mom, I thought you'd left already," he said, stopping short at finding her sitting in the office.

He walked over to her and kissed her on the cheeks.

"Hi, son," she said, lifting her cheeks to

his lips. She then added, "No, I'm still here. Is Tracy still in?"

"No, she just left. She's checking out another house for us, and before you know it, we'll be out of here, and you and Dad will have the place back to yourself."

He sat down in the chair next to her. She wore a grey pantsuit that Matthew had never seen her in before.

"There's no rush. Take your time. It's good having both of you here."

"Thanks, Mom," Matthew said, smiling over at her.

Mr. Ward walked into the office.

"Good morning, Matthew," he said and walked to the other side of the desk.

He sat and took out of a drawer the brown envelope he had in his hand last night. He rested it on his desk.

"Morning, Dad," Matthew replied, "you wanted me to stop by before entering the office?"

"Yes, yes, I did," he said before inhaling loudly.

Mr. Ward slowly pushed himself out of the chair and walked to the sliding door. Opened white horizontal wooden shutters hang there. He backed his family.

Matthew glanced at his mom. She sat rigidly, and this body position instantly transported him back to his childhood days, and his heart involuntarily skipped a beat.

Something's wrong, he thought. *I'm in some sort of trouble.*

He quickly raced through his memory, trying to retrace his steps and pull out what he might have done recently to disappoint them. His father turned from the door and returned to his seat behind the desk. He inhaled quietly before looking up at his son and asking, "Have you ever met someone named Janice Shepherd, son?"

"Janice Shepherd, Janice Shepherd, no, I've never heard that name before. You mean Shepherd as in James Shepherd, the copy typist?"

"This is not someone from your present. It is someone from your past. Someone you might have known shortly before going to college," Mr. Ward said.

"Probably, but right now, it doesn't sound familiar." Matthew frowned slightly.

Mr. Ward took up the brown envelope from his desk and handed it to him. Matthew half rose from the chair and took it from him. His parents exchanged glances as he opened the envelope and pulled a large photograph halfway out. Matthew gulped down saliva. He returned the photo to the envelope and rested it on the desk.

"I can't say for sure, but she looks like someone I'd known from high school or something," he said, trying to keep his voice steady. He cleared his throat. *I can stare down grown men and women in boardrooms, but why can't I do the same with my parents? I'm not a child anymore.*

"Why are you asking me about her? What's this all about?" he asked.

"About a week after you left for college overseas," Mr. Ward began, "your mother and I got a call from a man called Thomas."

"Yes," Mrs. Ward joined in, "he wanted a face-to-face conversation with us. That's how he'd put it."

"Your mom tried to find out what he wanted on the phone, but all he would say was that it was about you and it was personal."

"After hearing that, I knew where he was going. It sounded like the situation you had with that girl a year or two before," Mrs. Ward said.

"So we told him to come here," Mr. Ward continued. "He brought someone he said was his sister, Janice Shepherd." He pointed at the envelope.

Matthew gripped the chair's handles.

"Sure enough," his mother continued, "she claimed she was pregnant."

Matthew swallowed hard and waited for his parents to continue their narrative, but they only stared at him.

"What did they say?" he asked, looking from one of them to the other.

His mouth had become dry, and he licked his lips. His parents glanced at each other.

"She told us that she was pregnant with your child, our grandchild," Mrs. Ward said with her eyes fixed on his face.

"But of course, we didn't believe her," Mr. Ward said, bracing back in his chair and crossing his arms across his chest.

Matthew slowly let out a breath he didn't realize he was holding, and his grip on the chair's arms slowly relaxed. Mrs. Ward slapped him on the back of his neck and jumped out of her chair. The unexpected slap stung, and he spun around in the chair to confront her. His nose flared.

"I verbally abused and degraded that poor child," his mother yelled.

"What are you talking about?" Matthew rubbed the back of his neck.

"She accused you of sexually assaulting her, son," Mr. Ward said.

Matthew's hand lifelessly dropped from his neck.

"Did you do that, Matthew?" Mr. Ward asked.

"It wasn't like that." Matthew raised his hand into the stop position.

Matthew rose from his chair and paced

the floor before he stopped to stand behind the chair. He gripped the back of it for support.

"I don't believe this," Mrs. Ward exclaimed, throwing her arms into the air.

Mr. Ward stood. "Then tell us what happened." He pushed the chair with the back of his knees and stepped out from behind the desk

"*Technically*, it was not sexual assault," Matthew said, looking from his dad to his mom, but he was not meeting their eyes.

His mother threw her arms in the air again before allowing them to land on her head. She turned away from him, then, in a fury, she turned around and rushed over to him. Her hand was in the air, ready to slap him when he caught it.

"Mom, please, stop hitting me. I'm not a little boy anymore," he said, holding her hand and meeting her eyes as his jaw clenched and unclenched.

She glared at him briefly before yanking her hand out of his grip. Then, turning around, she walked around to her chair and sat down.

"What do you mean by *technically*?" his father asked. His father put air quotes around "technically."

Matthew drew himself to his full height and, taking a deep breath, slowly let it out.

He walked around to his chair and sat beside his mother, and his father regained his seat.

"I had a tougher time dealing with Michael's death than I was letting on," Matthew began, "we were so close, and even after eight months of his passing, it still felt as though it was only yesterday." He looked at both of his parents, and they were perfectly still. "So, when three of my friends came up with a business idea, I agreed to be a part of it."

"What business idea?" Mr. Ward asked, "I don't remember you coming to us with a business idea."

"They told me that there were many women out there who would pay guys to come to their homes and have sex with them and not just plain sex... rough sex," Matthew avoided his parents' eyes.

They stared at him.

"I wasn't sure about being a part of it, but after going on my first job, just to try it out, everything went according to plan, and so I continued," he said.

"Wait a minute, are you saying you were a male prostitute?" Mrs. Ward asked.

"Kind of, yes." He loosened his tie.

"What do you mean by *kind of?*" Mr. Ward asked.

"It also involved some role-playing,"

"What do you mean? Stop beating around the bush and give us some plain answers," Mr. Ward said.

Matthew cleared his throat. "All the women had this fantasy of being … sexually assaulted."

"What?" Mrs. Ward exclaimed, "I can't believe what I'm hearing in my ears today."

"That's what they wanted, and everything went well every time I went on a job," he quickly responded.

His parents stared at him.

"Then the job with Janice Shepherd came up."

"Wait a minute," Mrs. Ward said, "how did these women get in touch with you and your friends?"

"I was not the contact man, and I didn't want to know how that part worked. I got photos of the women, their names, address to go to, the date and time to arrive and some other special instructions."

"And this is how it went with Janice Shepherd?" Mr. Ward asked.

"Yes, well, kind of."

"What do you mean by that, now?" Mr. Ward asked, exasperated.

"Wait a minute," Mrs. Ward said, raising her right hand into the stop position, "You said that woman hired you, but Janice Shepherd was a teenager. She was sixteen years old. She was not an adult."

"What do you mean? My notes said that

she had just turned eighteen. All of the jobs that I did were with adults. We weren't pedophiles. She must have lied about her age."

His mother murmured under her breath.

"I didn't even want to take this job, but the guys begged me to do it because they were busy. It was going to be my last job before leaving to go to college in Canada. So, in the end, I gave in and did it."

"Are you saying this girl paid you to come to her house?" Mr. Ward asked.

"Yes. As usual, I was given the instruction package and entered the house using the house key she gave us. I did everything in the instruction package, all of it." Matthew shifted in his chair.

"Since she hired you, why would she now turn around and cry rape?" Mrs. Ward asked.

"I don't know," Matthew replied, lifting and dropping his hands.

"Okay, okay," she said, "while you were carrying out these... instructions, did she tell you to stop at any time?"

"She did, but..."

"What?" his mother exclaimed.

"It was a part of the job. I was to play along with it, or we wouldn't get paid or hired again."

"What am I hearing in my ears today?" his mother squealed, throwing her hands forcefully through the air.

"Michael was dead, and no matter what I did, I couldn't stop the pain I was feeling, but when I was working, it helped to stop the pain for a little while," Matthew said pleadingly.

Mrs. Ward shook her head in disgust.

"You should have come to us. We would have helped you," Mrs. Ward said.

Matthew nodded. "I know you don't approve of what I did, and I'm not asking you to either, but the fact is, I did not assault her like she said I did. She hired me."

"Are you sure that she hired you, son?" Mr. Ward asked.

"Yes, she did. After the job ended, I will admit that, for a brief second, I thought I'd entered the wrong house, so I bolted from there and called the guys and told them what happened, but they assured me I did go to the right house, and she hired us. Then she paid us the remainder the following day and even left a large tip for me."

His mother's mouth dropped open, but she quickly closed it.

"And what about protection? Didn't you use protection on these... rendezvous?" Mr. Ward asked.

"Of course I did. I always did."

"Then what happened here?" Mrs. Ward asked.

"What do you mean?"

"She said that she was pregnant," Mr. Ward said.

"She was lying or pregnant with someone else's child, but either way, she was looking to recount what she paid for and a big payday," Matthew said.

His parents looked at each other, and Matthew got up from the chair.

"So you see," he said, pushing his hands into his pants pocket, "I'm not a rapist, and I'm not the father of her child. Maybe this was a set-up from the beginning by her and her brother. Hey, perhaps this guy is not even her brother. He could be the father of the child!" His parents continued to look at each other.

"Besides, you know my medical condition," he added.

"Yes, but the doctors said there is nothing physically wrong with you. You should be able to have children," Mrs. Ward said.

"Yes, I know, but in this case, they're wrong," he said, pulling his right hand out of his pocket and rubbing his forehead. Then suddenly hit by a revelation, he said, "Wait a minute... Is this about the adoption? I thought you guys were on board with us about adopting?"

"Of course, we are on board with this," Mrs. Ward said.

"Then why are you asking me about this

now? It happened over twenty or so years ago. Why are you bringing all of this up now?"

His father cleared his throat, and his mother crossed her legs.

"When Miss Shepherd and her brother came here, they were not trying to shake us down for money. They wanted us to find someone to adopt the baby when they were born," his father said.

"What?" Matthew exclaimed.

"Oh yes, that's what they said, but we sent them packing and hired a private investigator to find out more about them, and we waited for them to make their second move," his mother said.

"But they never did, and we never looked at the private investigator's report," his father added.

"That is until we found out that you're infertile or whatever is going on in your body," his mom added.

Matthew returned to his seat.

"You know how much we wanted grandchildren," she continued, "and to say the least, this news hit us hard."

"I thought you said you were on board with the adoption."

"The same day you told us about your situation, I came into this office to look for an old file, and I came across the P.I's report, so I read it and then showed it to your mother."

"And after I read it, we decided to hire another PI to find out what happened to the child she was carrying," his mother added.

"What?" Matthew asked, "Why?"

"Why do you think that?" she asked, with a trace of anger.

"I don't know. You would have to tell me. I don't understand any of what you're saying."

"The P.I. confirmed that she was pregnant, and although she had a boyfriend, the two of them had broken up two months before, and she did not have another boyfriend up to that point. We still didn't believe you'd attack her as she'd claimed, but we thought that maybe the child could be yours," his father said.

"Why?"

"What do you mean by why? You'd sworn to us that you didn't sleep with that girl the first time, but that wasn't the truth, was it?" his mother said as her anger rose.

Matthew dropped his head.

His mother inhaled loudly and threw her hands into the air.

"We've found the child, and he is your son. He is our grandchild," his father said quietly as a smile broke across his face.

"What?" Matthew exclaimed as his head flew up.

"You have a son, Matthew," his dad

said, still smiling.

"What are you talking about? I cannot have children."

"No," his mom said, "that's not what the doctors said. They said they could not find any medical reasons for you not being able to have a child."

"But I used a condom."

"Well, this time, you must have not used it correctly, or it burst or something," Mrs. Ward responded.

Matthew opened his mouth to say something but slammed it shut.

"The new P.I. found him," his father said.

"Where is he? Who is he?" Matthew asked, bewildered.

"You've met him already," his dad said.

"I did. When? Who is he?" he asked, looking at both his parents.

"He is James Shepherd, the copy typist at Glen's, the one you asked me about last night," his father said.

Matthew sank deeper into his chair while holding onto his head. "Do you know for sure that he's my son? Did you get a paternity test done?"

"Yes, it's all in the P.I.'s report," Mr. Ward said.

"Does he know about us? Who adopted him?" Matthew asked after a few minutes of silence.

"No one adopted him," his mother said, "she never gave him up for adoption."

Matthew leapt out of the chair.

"You see, that proves it. I didn't assault this girl. She hired us," Matthew said, almost shouting.

"What do you mean?" his mother asked.

"If I'd assaulted her as she said, why would she keep the baby? I know it's illegal to have an abortion in this country, but people still do it, especially since she said I assaulted her."

His parents looked at each other.

"I don't believe this," Matthew said, pulling off his tie and throwing it on his vacated chair. Then, he looked at his parents and asked, "Does he know about us, about me? Is that why he applied to the copy typist job?"

"We don't think so," Mr. Ward said.

"But it is still possible, right?" Matthew rubbed the sides of his head with his slender fingers.

"It is possible, but we don't think he knows who we are because, as you would remember, we only recently released the information that we are the new owners of Glen's Magazine. He had already applied for the job before we made the announcement," Mr. Ward said.

"And two days ago, we had a face-to-face with him, and he treated us only as his employers," his mother said.

"You should have seen him, son. He's quite a young man, and his resume is outstanding," Mr. Ward said, and for the second time since entering the home office, he smiled. Then he added, "He's going places, son, and with our help, he'll get there."

"When would you tell him about us, about me?" Matthew asked, folding his arms across his chest.

"We would like you to do that," Mr. Ward said, standing and pushing his hands into his pocket.

"I'll have to tell Tracy first, and I don't know how she'll take this," Matthew said, unfolding his arms and rubbing his forehead.

Unexpectedly, a soft knock came on the office door, and Matthew jumped, and his parents frowned at him.

"Come in," his father commanded, and the butler, dressed in his customary white and black uniform, entered the room. He had aged well throughout the years.

"I'm sorry to interrupt you," he said, "but Mr. Weebly, the next-door neighbour, is at the front door and demanding to speak to you, sir."

"Alright, thanks, George," Mr. Ward said, glancing at his watch, "give me five minutes and then send him in."

"Yes, sir," George said, then bowing slightly, he left the room, closing the door behind him.

"I didn't realize it was this late already," his father said, looking down at his watch again. Then, while he picked up the folder from his desk and returned it to the drawer under his desk, he added, "After you've talked with Tracy, let us know what you've decided to do but don't take too long because we have a grandson, and we don't want to miss out on another minute of his life."

"Okay, Dad," Matthew said, grabbing his tie from the chair and heading for the door.

"I have several errands to take care of," Matthew heard his mother say, and they both walked out of the office.

CHAPTER 13
AN INVITATION

James breathed a sigh of relief as he read the note from his mom.

After discovering his conception, he didn't know how to face her the following morning. The night before, when his uncle followed him into his bedroom, he'd sat silently on his bed. Then, after several minutes, he'd looked at him and asked, "Would you like to pray with me, James?"

"I don't know what to say. I thought I knew who I was, but now..." James said, throwing his hands into the air and letting them fall onto his bed.

"You already know who you are, James. None of this changes that."

"Doesn't it, uncle? I now know I'm a constant reminder to my mom of the worst day in her life, and that changes everything. That changes me," James said, choking on unshed tears.

"She loves you, James. We all do."

"But how could she, though?"

"Because she chooses to. She chooses to love you, James, and even though your world suddenly seems to be upside down, you have a family who loves you and is here for you, but above all, Jesus loves you, and He will bring you through this. Allow Him to do so," Uncle Thomas said, laying a hand on his shoulder.

James' thoughts kept him silent for a few minutes.

"I can't pray right now, uncle, but you can go ahead and do so."

"Okay."

He prayed and then left the room.

James returned to the present and glanced at the note in his hand. He whispered, "Please help me, Lord. Please help me." Then he said, "I love you too, Mom," in response to her, "I love you," in the note.

I can't go to work today, James, though, taking a sizeable black teacup from the overhead cupboard.

"But others are depending on me," he said to the cup before putting it on the countertop. "Granted, I practically did all of my work yesterday. So, there wouldn't be much to do today."

He poured the steaming water from the black electric kettle.

"Who am I kidding? Others are depending on me. My problems are not their fault."

He slumped his shoulders, then looked at his watch.

There's still time to write my resignation letter before going in.

He poured milk into his cup.

A few hours later, James was at work, and to his relief, his bosses were not there, and they did not enter the building for the entire day. He buried himself in his work, trying to keep his mind from thinking about his personal life.

At the end of the workday, there were no papers on his desk, and his stomach was loudly rumbling because he had skipped his lunch hour.

That evening, dinner with his mom was quiet, partly due to their empty stomachs. They were eating some of last night's leftovers.

"I didn't realize I was so hungry," his mom said, putting down her fork.

"Me too. I skipped lunch today because I wanted to finish all the work on my desk."

"Do you do that often?" she asked, putting a forkful of food into her mouth.

"Do what? Skip lunch?"

She nodded.

"Oh, no. Today was the first time."

"Okay," she said, nodding.

He had finished eating several minutes earlier.

"I didn't skip lunch, but I didn't eat anything substantial, either," she said.

James nodded as he dropped the two pieces of ice from his glass into his mouth. Silence, like the elephant in the room, fell between them.

"James, do you want to talk with me about it?" his mom asked, breaking the silence.

"I do, but not right now, Mom," he replied, silently pleading with her to give him some room.

"I don't want this to destroy our relationship." She looked at him.

He reached for her hand on the table and squeezed it gently but briefly.

"That's never going to happen, Mom, because, even in your darkest hours, you choose to have and keep me. I love you, and nothing will change that." His voice cracked.

"I love you too, son," she replied as her tears gathered.

"I just need some time, that's all," he said pleadingly.

"Okay, okay," she said, blinking away the tears, "I'll give you some room. I've had years to deal with this, but you've only had a few hours." She smiled, but it did not reach her eyes.

He smiled, squeezing her hand again and letting go of it.

"Do you have a new client?" he asked.

Thrown a little off guard at the sudden change in the subject, she blinked her eyes rapidly for a few seconds before chuckling.

"You saw the signs, nah?"

He nodded.

Janice chuckled again and told him about her new client. As she spoke, James' thoughts drifted to the resignation letter he'd given to the receptionist. She was going to pass it on to the Human Resources department. The upcoming two weeks would be his last there, and he was hoping to leave without having any more interactions with the Wards. He thought about quitting the job at the end of the week, but he knew that would not be fair to his co-workers.

In the next two weeks, the magazine was turning thirty years old. So, in recognition of that, a special edition was coming out to mark the occasion. The entire staff was working hard on it, and James did not want to leave them in a lurch.

I wonder if the Wards know who I am. Is this why they hired me and have now offered me the scholarship? Oh, what does it matter?

He threw his thoughts out of his mind as he focused on what his mom said.

On Thursday, the workday slowly passed, and on Friday, while sitting at his desk, he glanced at his watch for the umpteen times.

He thought that there was only one more hour to go before the weekend. Then, by the door, the cream-corded phone rang.

"I'll get it," Simon said, getting to his feet.

"Okay," James said, glancing up at him.

"Glen's Magazine, Simon speaking."

He was silent for a few seconds before saying, "Will do, and you are welcome."

"The big boss wants you to come to his office in the next five minutes," Simon said after putting down the receiver.

James felt his heart drop in his chest.

Lord, help me, please.

"Since the boss seems to like you so much, don't forget to put in a good word for me." Simon returned to the desk.

"You don't need me, Simon. Your work speaks for itself. You do excellent work. You'll be climbing the ladder faster than I can catch up," James replied as he got up.

"I will, wouldn't I?" He smiled broadly and shook his shoulders in a dance move.

James laughed as he headed for the door.

James felt awful about waiting until his last two weeks were over before telling Simon he was leaving, but he thought that would be the best way to handle it.

He took a deep breath and slowly let it out

before knocking on Oliver Ward's office door. The command to enter came immediately, and when he obeyed, he found his boss sitting behind his desk.

"Ah, James, come in, come in," Mr. Ward said, rising from his chair.

He stretched out his hand, and James hesitantly took it.

"Sit, sit." With a wave of his hand, Mr. Ward offered him the chair in front of the desk.

"Thank you," James said, sitting.

After he resumed his seat, he said, "Mrs. Ward and I would like to invite you to our home for dinner tomorrow. We know it is a little late, but we hope you can come."

James opened his mouth, but nothing came out, so he closed it. He briefly smiled as he wrestled with whether or not to tell him what his mother told him about his birth.

"Would six o'clock be a good time?" Mr. Ward asked. Then he stretched out his arm with a card on it. "Here. I've written the address on the back of it."

"Thank you," James said as he took the card and looked at the address.

"But, if you prefer, I can get my driver to pick you up instead." Mr. Ward looked at him over the top of his glasses.

The address looked like a residential area, telling James that public transportation would not take him to the house. Therefore, he would be walking part of the way there. Nevertheless, he did not want the Wards or their driver to come to his home. He did not want them anywhere near his mom.

"Thank you. But that's okay. I'll find my way there."

"Okay, good," Mr. Ward said, getting up.

James rose, too.

"Until tomorrow, then," Mr. Ward said, stretching his hand for a shake.

"Yes, thanks," James said, shaking hands before putting the card into his blue-striped shirt's top pocket and heading for the door.

As he returned to his working area, he mentally kicked himself there.

What was that? Why did I say yes instead of no? Madness. He quietly signed as he entered the room and sat behind his desk. *I'll have to tell Mom.*

So, after returning home that evening, he told her about the dinner invitation.

"Okay," she said.

"Okay?" James asked, raising his eyebrow.

She nodded.

"Do you think they know who I am?" he asked.

She cleared her throat. "They might."

She was sitting in the long chair in the

living room, and several books were on the chair and the coffee table. She wore a pink and white T-shirt with "January Island" at the front and black three-quarter cotton pants.

"Yeah, I was thinking so," James said, nodding thoughtfully. He then leaned on the wall that led to his bedroom. "Do you think they are planning to bring it up tomorrow?"

She looked up from the book her eyes had strayed to and answered, "They might."

"I'm sorry, Mom."

"Sorry for what?"

"For putting you through this. I mean, these people are your attacker's parents, and here I am, talking to you about them and going to have dinner with them. What kind of a person am I?" Tears flooded his eyes, but he quickly blinked them away.

"Come here," she said, pushing away the books and clearing an area for him to sit.

He sat, and she embraced him tightly for a few seconds, and he returned her hug. She released him but held his face between her hands.

"You are James Mark Shepherd, and you are my son. You already know who you are. I know you have a lot to deal with right now, but you will get through this. We both will. Okay?"

"Okay," he said, nodding.

She kissed him on the forehead.

"Now, Stacy called earlier and left a message for you on the answering machine."

"She did?" James asked, his eyes brightening with pleasure.

"Yes. How much longer before she returns?"

"About six more weeks to go. I miss her and Sammy so much. I can't believe both of them are away at the same time. Stacy is on her yearly visit to her dad in Canada, and Sammy is in Belize doing missionary work."

"Yeah, I miss them too, but before you know it, they will return." His mom smiled slightly.

"Yeah, I guess," he said, getting up, "I'll let you get back to work, and I'll listen to Stacy's message, then tidy up before dinner."

"Before you go," Janice said, lightly holding his arm until he sat down again, "have you told Stacy and Sammy about Matthew Ward?"

"No, not as yet. I think I want to wait until they get back. I don't feel comfortable telling them something like this on the phone."

"Yeah, I understand. Good, good." She smiled over at him.

He returned the smile.

"Okay," Janice said, "let me not keep you any longer. Go and listen to your message."

"Okay," James said, getting up, "what's

for dinner? I'll set the table after taking a shower."

She nodded and told him before he disappeared behind the walls with the phone.

CHAPTER 14
DINNER

The following afternoon, James travelled on the public bus to as far as it would take him, and he walked the rest of the way to the Wards' residence.

He wore long dark blue pants and a white long-sleeve shirt, keeping his body cooled against the breeze. He was walking for about fifteen minutes when he entered their neighbourhood, and although the sun had departed and darkness had taken its place, it was not difficult for him to find where they lived.

In golden numbers, the house numbers were on the triangular arch at the entrance to the porch. The grass on the lawn was green and cut low, and sprinklers were refreshing it. A long, semi-curved concrete walkway that led to the front door formed a Y that led to the house's sides.

The garages are probably there, James thought as he walked down the walkway.

Pink, white, and blue flowers surrounded the front of the extended patio, and lights from the roof, walls and the ground lit up the house and some of the walkways. The modernly designed home displayed concrete and stone. Large Bay and Stationary windows also surrounded the front of the house.

Wow. If this house is impressive on the outside, what does it look like inside?

He walked the few circular white concrete steps to the top and pressed the buzzer.

After a few minutes of standing there, a man who looked to be in his early sixties and was dressed in a black and white suit opened the door.

"Good evening," James said, smiling, "is this the Wards' residence?"

The man, slightly taller than James, looked down at him, and to James' surprise, the man's mouth dropped open, but he quickly closed it and said, "You are almost the spitting image of your mother."

"My mom? You know my mom?" James asked, raising his eyebrows.

The man's right index finger quickly went to his lips, and he tapped them twice. He smiled, then said, "Please, come in, Mr. Shepherd. The Wards are expecting you."

He stepped aside, allowing him to enter, and the first thing he noticed was the island he was standing on in the foyer. His eyes then travelled to the house's elegant black and white pillars. A flared stairway led to an upper floor and even more elegance than he'd ever seen in a private home.

"Come this way, please," the man said, leading him into a large family room.

The room was just as beautiful as the other parts he'd seen.

"Would you like something to drink?" he asked.

James opened his mouth to refuse, but the thirty minutes of walking had left him thirsty, so he said, "Can I have some water, please?"

"Very well," he replied and walked deeper into the room and poured a glass of water from a crystal-clear glass pitcher on a brown table in the far corner.

"Ice?" he asked over his shoulder.

"Yes, thanks."

A few seconds later, James had guzzled down the water.

"The Wards will be down soon. Please have a seat when you're ready," the man said before leaving the room.

James was now standing next to the brown table in the far corner and was on his third glass of water when Mr. Ward entered the room.

"Ah... James. You made it."

"Yes, sir," he replied, putting down the half-empty glass before shaking the outstretched hand.

Mrs. Ward then entered, and for the umpteen time, James wondered if they had also invited their son and his wife. He knew that their son and his wife had no children because this was in the magazine, which featured the new owners of Glen Magazine.

I wonder why they do not have any children.

The Wards sat in one of the white leather chairs and invited him to sit before asking about his day. From there, the conversation led to other things, which included the cool night air.

They were there for about fifteen minutes when the man who answered the door returned to the room and announced, "Dinner is ready, Mr. and Mrs. Ward."

"Thanks, George," Mr. Ward said.

"Come along, James," Mrs. Ward said, leading them out of the room.

He led James to a room with a nine-piece, dark finish, mahogany dining table. A sparkling glass chandelier, the shape of a bowl, was hanging above the table's centre. The table faced a large bay window with its multi-colour undrawn curtains and two dark finish mahogany hutches. Several paintings and family photos adorned the walls.

Various plates, glasses and utensils sat on the table. Foods and dishes that James had never eaten before were also there.

"Here, James, sit next to me," Mr. Ward said, pulling out the chair on the left side of the head of the table facing the bay window.

"Thank you," James said, taking the chair and sitting in it.

Mr. Ward sat, and Mrs. Ward sat on his right side.

"Sorry we're late," an unfamiliar woman's voice said. "I was having a little trouble deciding on what to wear."

James' eyes followed the voice, and a tall, beautiful, light-brown-skinned woman and Matthew Ward entered the dining room. James envisioned himself rushing from the table and striking Matthew Ward several times before leaving the house. However, his body remained rooted in the chair, and his thoughts were interrupted when Mrs. Ward said, "You're right on time."

She's probably Tracy Ward, James thought. She sat next to him, and Matthew sat next to his mother. Tracy Ward looked, then smiled at him before frowning briefly. She stretched her hand to him and said, "Hi, I am Tracy."

"Please to meet you," James said, taking her hand, "I'm James."

He let go of her hand and glanced over at Matthew, who was whispering something to his mother. His eyes then travelled to the food on the table, and his stomach rumbled like thunder. He tensed and hoped that no one else heard it.

"Excuse me," James whispered. *Just in case someone did heard.*

"Did you say something?" Mr. Ward asked, looking at him.

Good, James thought, *he didn't hear it.*

"Everything looks delicious, Dad," Tracy said.

"Yes, our chef is an excellent cook," Mr. Ward replied, turning to look at her.

"Let's give God thanks," Mrs. Ward said.

James was momentarily surprised because he had the impression that this family did not pray, but he closed his eyes, and she prayed, "Lord, thank you for the bounty you set before us tonight. Amen."

"Amen," was echoed around the table.

James had never eaten lobsters and didn't know what to do with some of the utensils. He glanced over at Matthew throughout the meal, and he was two steps behind him in whatever he was using and eating. They ate silently throughout the dinner, and when the meal was over, they went to the entertainment room, where Mr. and Mrs. Ward played a few games of pools against their son and daughter-in-law. A pool stick was offered to James when they entered the room. However, he quickly declined, explaining that he did not know how to play the game.

"I can teach you," Matthew said, "It's easy to learn."

"Thanks, but that's okay."

"Okay, why don't you try the gaming machine instead," Mrs. Ward suggested, smiling at him.

"Yeah, that's a good idea," he replied, heading towards the built-in machine.

Dark brown carpet graced the floor, and a light brown oak table with four chairs, a foosball table, a brown leather chair and a wooden bookshelf were also in there.

James found a car racing game on the machine, and he was so involved in it that he didn't notice when the older Mr. Ward came to stand behind his chair.

"You beat the top score!" he exclaimed.

"Yeah, I killed it!" James exclaimed, swirling around in the chair to look at him.

Mr. Ward was beaming from ear to ear.

Suddenly feeling hot, James cleared his throat and turned back to the game as he said, "I mean, yes, I did a few minutes ago."

Mr. Ward laughs boisterously.

"Good for you," Mrs. Ward said, joining them in laughter, tapping James on the shoulder.

Their laughter brought Matthew and Tracy over.

"What's so funny, Dad?"

"James is now the new record holder in Cars of the Ages," he said as his laughter reduced to a chuckle.

"Your cou..." Mrs. Ward began, looking at James.

She coughed, suddenly clearing her throat.

"One of Matthew's cousins wouldn't be too happy about that. He thinks he's the king of this game," Mr. Ward said to James.

"I keep telling him that there's always someone else out there who is better than you, but he wouldn't listen to me," Matthew said, shaking his head.

"I got it now," Tracy suddenly exclaimed. "From the moment I met you, you kept reminding me of someone, but I couldn't pinpoint who it was."

Silence suddenly flew across the room as everyone held their breath.

"I've got it now. You look like one of the security guards I saw at the Real Estate office earlier this week," she said, pointing an index finger at James before snapping two of her fingers together.

Matthew and his dad quietly exhaled while Mrs. Ward slowly shook her head.

"Do you have a grandmother who is a security guard?" she asked James.

"Yes," James replied.

But I've never met her, he thought, but

he kept that thought to himself.

"I knew it," Tracy exclaimed, smiling, "I'm good with faces."

"You certainly are, honey," Matthew said, smiling at her as he threw his arm around her shoulders.

"Tracy," Mrs. Ward said, taking her by the upper arm, "why don't you join Dad and me in the library while Matthew and James discuss a few things."

"Yeah, sure." Tracy replied, a little disconcerted, "But I thought this was not a business dinner."

"Yes, Mom," Matthew said, giving both of his parents a questioning look.

His mother returned the gaze, and it was a familiar one. He said to Tracy: "Go ahead, honey. I'll join you as soon as we're finished."

"Okay," Tracy said, allowing Mrs. Ward to lead her out of the room with Mr. Ward following.

"Would you like something to drink?" Matthew asked after the door was closed by his dad.

"Yes, thanks. Do you have any Sprite?" James replied, realizing that his throat had suddenly gone dry.

Matthew walked to the far corner of the room and pulled open a cupboard door that exposed the inside of a small refrigerator.

"Catch," Matthew said, throwing a can

of Sprite to him.

"Thanks." James opened it and drank most of it before removing the can from his mouth.

"Please, sit with me," Matthew said after taking a mouthful of Coca-Cola from his can.

James watched as Matthew walked over to the long brown leather chair before walking over to the table and chairs directly opposite the leather chair. He pulled out a chair and sat down. James took another mouthful of Sprite. Matthew lifted an eyebrow, and a slight smile appeared at the corner of his lips, but he said nothing.

James raised his eyebrows at him.

"James, do you know who I am?" Matthew asked.

"Yes," James replied slowly. "You are one of my bosses."

Matthew smiled. "No, I do not mean that."

"Then I know what you mean." James nodded.

"Okay," Matthew said, looking at him. "Then there's no way around this, so I'm simply going to say it." He paused. "I recently found out from my parents that they hired a private investigator whose reports say you're my son."

"Okay," James instantly replied as he nodded again.

"Did your mother tell you who I was then?"

"Yes, she told me a few days ago."

"Only a few days ago? You didn't know who I was before then?" Matthew asked with skepticism in his voice.

"No."

Matthew waited for him to continue, but James said nothing else.

"What did she say to you about me?" Matthew asked after taking a deep breath.

"She told me that you assaulted her." James' jaws stiffened, and his grip around the can tightened.

"But I didn't assault her," was Matthew's instant reply as he jumped forward to the edge of the chair.

"To tell you the truth, it's only God who's keeping me from striking you down," James said in a low, calm voice.

The can in his hand was dented, but its liquid did not spill.

"I can understand that." Matthew nodded. "If I were in your shoes, I would want to do the same thing. I am just asking you to give me a chance to tell you my side of things, and I know that you want to allow me to do so because you would not have come otherwise."

James slowly exhaled and drained the can to his lips before resting it on the table.

"Some friends of mine came up with the idea of hiring ourselves out to women," Matthew said.

"You mean they wanted to be male prostitutes," James said.

"Well..., yes, but we did not see it like that. We saw it as a way of..., Yes."

He put the Coca-Cola can to his mouth and emptied it.

"Mom said she never hired you."

"That's what she said to me, and for a moment, I panicked, and I believed her, but my friends assured me that she did hire us," Matthew said.

Matthew stood, walked over to a cupboard, and opened the door before dropping the empty can. He returned to his seat.

"My mom was only sixteen," James said after Matthew returned to the chair. "Why would she hire you, and where would she have gotten the money from?"

"My notes said she was eighteen, James, and I don't mean to be cruel, but if she didn't hire me, why didn't she give you up for adoption?"

There was a moment of silence before James said, "Well, you are cruel. Nevertheless, why would my mother lie?"

"You would have to ask her that question."

"Look," James said, getting to his feet,

"this is getting us nowhere."

"Please, just give me a chance," Matthew said, jumping to his feet.

"Why? What more can you say to me about this? You are saying one thing, and my mom is saying something else, and the only thing that we can all agree on is that I am here." James folded his arms across his chest.

"That's true, but I'm not talking only about that. I would like you to give my family and me a chance to get to know each other," Matthew said.

James stared at him.

"I'm not a rapist and certainly not a pedophile, James," Matthew said.

"And my mother is not a liar. Look, this is not going to work. Thanks for dinner; it was enjoyable, but I must go now."

He headed for the closed door.

"You don't have to leave right now," Matthew asked, with his arms wide open.

"Of course I do because there's nothing else to say," James said over his shoulder.

"We can get past this, James. I want you to be a part of my life."

"Yes, but that's just it. I don't know how to get past it."

He reached the door.

"Give it some time; don't make any decisions right now."

James stopped, briefly thought about Matthew's words, and opened the door.

"Let me walk you to the front door," Matthew said, quickening his steps to catch up with him.

They walked in silence through the house, which stunned him even now, and when they stepped outside, the cool night air, like a damped blanket on a cold night, wrapped itself around him, and he rubbed his arms to warm his body. Crickets filled the air with their dance.

"It has gotten a lot cooler," he said, lifting his shirt collar.

"It's nice out here," Matthew inhaled deeply.

"Bye," James said as the breeze gently kissed his cheeks, and he yawned.

"Excuse me," he said before walking down the steps.

He stretched and yawned again.

"Where did you park your car?" Matthew asked, still walking behind him.

"Car? I don't have a car."

"You don't?" Matthew raised his eyebrows. "How do you get around? Did you take a taxi to get here?"

"No," James said, "I usually catch the bus, and I took it to get here."

"But buses don't drive in this area," Matthew said, looking around as though seeking confirmation for his words.

The crickets continued their dance.

"Yes, I know. I rode the bus as far as it would take me and walked the rest of the way here." James looked at his watch. It was ten-thirty.

"Come back inside," Matthew said, retracing his steps up the stairs, "I'll call you a taxi."

"I can't take a taxi. I don't have enough money."

"Don't worry about it," Matthew called over his shoulder, "I'll take care of it."

He disappeared inside.

James sat on the stairs instead of following him back into the house.

"Oh, Lord," he silently prayed. "This is so difficult. How can I have a relationship with him and my mother at the same time? I can't do it. Oh Lord, please help me."

Matthew returned, sat beside him, and said, "The taxi would be here in about five to ten minutes."

"Thanks."

"Here," he said, giving him a bill.

James hesitated for a few seconds, but as another yawn threatened to escape from him, he reached out and took it.

"Thank you," he said, and without looking at the money, he stretched out his right leg and, leaning slightly backwards, pushed it into his pants pocket.

"I grew up in this house, and I can't tell you the last time I've sat on these steps," Matthew said, stretching his legs and looking around him. "My brother Michael and I used to run around here all the time."

"Michael?" James asked, glancing at him, "I didn't know you have a brother."

"I did. But he died about twenty-one years ago."

"Oh. I'm sorry to hear that. How did Michael die? If you don't mind me asking?"

"A drunk driver killed him."

"I'm sorry for your loss," James whispered.

"Thank you."

Silence fell between them.

"Michael was older than me by two years, and we were very close. He was on his way to one of my cricket matches the day he died."

"Oh. That's sad."

"Yes, thanks," Matthew replied, sighing heavily. He cleared his throat. "After he was gone, my love for the game disappeared. I couldn't play a game without thinking about him. For a little while after he was gone, I kept thinking that he was in the stands, cheering me on. He never missed any of my matches, and after every game, he would say to me, 'You're going all the way to the top, Matthew, all the way.'"

Headlights suddenly appeared in the distance, and within minutes, a yellow taxi pulled up in the driveway to their left.

"The taxi's here," James said as he slowly rose to his feet.

Matthew stood up, too.

"Thank you," James said, patting his pocket where he had pushed the money in.

"Don't mention it. It was a pleasure having you here, James. Thanks for coming."

James nodded, then headed for the back door of the taxi. When he opened the door, a yellow light eliminated the cab, and the bald driver asked, "Where to?"

James told him, and as the driver left the driveway, James saw Matthew was still standing on the stairs, and he was waving at him. James returned the wave, and a few minutes later, he fell asleep in the taxi.

Sometime later, the taxi driver woke him.

"Sorry," James said, "I didn't realize how tired I was."

"Which house?"

After rubbing his eyes and yawning, he replied. "It's the cream and white one on your left, over there,"

"Okay," the driver said, driving to and stopping in front of a chain-linked gate. The fence surrounded the entire house.

James stretched out his right leg and pulled out the money. He'd assumed that Matthew had given him fifty dollars, but as he looked at the money before giving it to the driver, he saw it was a one hundred dollar bill.

"I'm sorry. I don't have anything smaller."

"Nah," the driver said, "I have enough change."

He paid his fare, the driver returned the change, and he left the taxi and entered his home with his keys.

At the Wards' residence, Matthew went to his father's home office and threw himself into the long black leather chair. He covered his face with his hands.

"Stupid, stupid, stupid," he said quietly. "I blew it."

He was lost in his thoughts for a few minutes before a small smile rose at the corner of his lips and soon engulfed his face.

"I have a son," he whispered. "I'm a father. Wow!"

Then, getting up, he went in search of Tracy.

James was having breakfast with his mom the following morning when she asked, "Was that a car I heard last night?"

She was chewing a piece of toasted bread.

"Yes, Matthew, I mean, Mr. Ward, the son, give me a hundred dollars to pay for it." James looked down at his scrambled eggs.

"Oh, I see. How was dinner?"

She sipped some of her hot tea.

"It was as good as it could have been. The Wards know about me. They admitted that I'm his child," he said, biting a piece of his toasted bread.

The teacup in his mother's hand shook, and some green tea spilled unto the see-through plastic-covered table.

"So he admitted to what he did to me?" she asked as her mouth fell open.

"No, Mom," James quickly replied, shaking his hand in front of his chest.

"Oh," she replied, like a deflated balloon. "What did he say happened then?"

James sighed quietly. "He said you hired him."

"I told him then, and I'm still saying it now: I did not hire him." Her voice rose as she hit the table with her fist. "You do believe me, don't you, James?"

"Of course, I believe you, Mom," he replied, reaching for her cuffed fist on the table.

"Okay, okay," she said, nodding and taking a deep breath to control her rising anger. "I'm sorry." She rested her other hand on his.

"You don't have to apologize for anything, Mom."

She nodded, then took another deep breath before slowly letting it out. Then, as though hit by a sudden realization, she said, "Eat, eat. You don't want to be late for church."

"Things will get better, Mom. It has to."

She smiled briefly before freeing his hand. Then, she reached out and touched his cheeks.

"Eat," she said again, and this time, he did.

Janice watched him eating for a few seconds before reaching for a tissue from the boat-shaped mahogany holder on the table and mopping up the spilled tea.

"Do you want to come to church with me today?" James asked.

"Not today, son, but maybe soon." Even though she smiled at him, it didn't reach her eyes.

"There's no time like the present," he said, bringing the teacup to his lips.

"I know, son, I know," she said, still smiling, "but maybe soon."

"Okay."

CHAPTER 15
TO A GYM

On Monday, James was tempted to stay at home.

They can't hold this against me, he thought. *Anyone in my position would do the same thing.*

Nevertheless, he went to work for the entire week and the next, and to his surprise, he did not see Matthew or his parents during the last two weeks of his employment.

What's going on here? One moment, they're inviting me to dinner, and the next, they're avoiding me like the plague. Well, what do I care? I've finished my time here; now it's time to move on. I now need to find another job that pays as well as this one.

So, on his last day there, he told Simon it was his last day.

"How can you do this to me, man?" Simon asked.

"What do you mean?"

"Why would you quit? We were working so well together!" Simon threw his hands in the air before they fell beside him, hitting the sides of his legs.

"I know, man, and I'm sorry, but I must move on for personal reasons."

"But you have only been here for about a month."

"Yep, I know."

Simon sighed heavily. "Well, I'm sorry to see you go. You are so good at this, and the bosses like you."

"Thanks," James said, and they shook hands.

"Well... All I'm asking is that the next person in that chair is just as good as you and not like the one before you."

James laughed.

"I'm serious," Simon said, "he didn't do the work, and it was also hard to get him to stop talking. The dude just wouldn't stop talking."

"Umm," James said, knowing how much Simon valued getting the work done and his personal space.

"Yeah," Simon said, nodding his head, and they both laughed.

As James was riding out his final weeks at work, he'd sent out resumes to other magazine houses, and he had three interviews on Monday, Tuesday, and Wednesday of the following week. He was looking forward to these interviews, and as he made his way home from the first job interview, he verbally kicked himself for some of the answers he had given in the meeting.

James mentally sighed as he stood at a bus stop, waiting for the bus to take him home. He was dressed in a light blue long-sleeve dress shirt tucked in long, black pants. As he stood there, a sparkling red Ferrari with its hood down stopped at the bus stop.

He better hope the cops don't see him, James thought as he moved his eyes from the car to the driver.

"Jump in," the driver, wearing dark sunglasses, called.

The driver was Matthew! James opened and closed his mouth like a flopping fish out of water. He took a small step back but couldn't stop a smile from forming. Embarrassed by the happiness, he hesitated to get into the car.

"I just want to spend some time with you, no pressure," Matthew said.

"I'll jump in if he doesn't," an elderly woman dressed in a purple and white dress called out. She was grinning from ear to ear, and she winked at James when he shifted his eyes to look at her. He laughed and shook his head at her.

James' shoulders relaxed. He looked up to see if any vehicle was coming his way before running to the other side of the car and jumping into the front passenger seat. Matthew rejoined the flowing traffic as soon as he'd buckled the seat belt. James turned to look behind him and saw the public bus pulling to a stop at the bus stop.

James looked around at the car's plush interior and exclaimed, "Wow, what a ride."

"Yes. You should have seen your grandfather's face when he first saw it. He said that it was an accident waiting to happen," Matthew said, smiling as he slowed behind a green Dodge Caravan.

James nodded but kept silent as he continued to look around the car.

"I know you do not have a car, but do you know how to drive?" Matthew asked after a few minutes of silence.

"No, but I will learn one of these days."

"Maybe I can teach you," Matthew glanced over at him.

"What are you doing in this area?" James asked as he looked at the dashboard.

"I was looking for you."

"For me? Why, why would you look for me here?" James looked over at him as he spoke.

"We own the magazine you just left."

"What?" James frowned slightly.

"Yes. Imagine my luck when I saw you walking out of the interview room," Matthew said as he overtook a blue car.

"Luck? There's no such thing. Oh, never mind. How many businesses does your family own?"

"A few," Matthew replied, smiling slightly.

"That's where you've been for the past few weeks?" James asked, trying to keep the disappointment he felt at not seeing him for the past two weeks out of his voice.

"There and other places because we thought giving you a little space would be best."

"When did you find out that I quit? Did you know that I had given in a resignation letter the evening I was over there?"

"No, not then. None of us knew then. We found out about it the following Tuesday."

"Okay," James nodded.

"We are just asking you to give us a chance," Matthew said, slowing down before stopping at another red light.

James exhaled heavily.

"What about Tracy?" he suddenly asked, as though the thought had just popped into his mind. "Have you told her about me?"

"Yes, I told her everything," Matthew replied, sighing heavily.

"Everything?"

"Yes, everything."

"Um, I'm surprised. I didn't think you would have told her everything."

"I didn't think so, too, but she's my wife, and I love her, and if I want my marriage and a relationship with you and us to work, I have to be honest with both of you."

"Mm. How is she taking it?"

"Better than I thought she would. She's an amazing person."

"Okay," James said, nodding his head.

"You don't think she's an amazing person?" A smile tugged at the side of his mouth.

"No, no," James quickly said, looking at Matthew as he shook his hand. "I didn't mean that. She seems nice. I just meant that I heard what you said."

Matthew laughed.

"You were just joking," James said as a chuckle escaped him.

"Yeah," Matthew admitted as he continued to laugh.

"Well, you got me," James admitted as he turned back to look at the road.

"James," Matthew said as the traffic light changed to green, "we're just asking you to give us a chance. My family and I want to get to know you."

"My mom said that your parents were callous to her."

"I know, and I'm sorry about that, but you must understand my parents' viewpoint. She had, and still accuses their son of a heinous crime I have not committed."

James did not reply but folded his arms across his chest.

They drove silently for a few minutes before Matthew asked, "How good are you at lifting weights?"

"What?" James asked as frown lines formed on his forehead.

"Weightlifting, how good are you?"

"Oh. I don't know. I've never lifted weights."

"Never?" Matthew asked, stealing a glance at him.

"No, never." James shook his head.

"Then how do you work out because even under those clothes, anyone can see that you're ripped and don't just tell me it's just youth?"

James smiled. "I ride my bicycle around the stadium every Saturday morning, and during the week, I do the regular push-ups, jump ropes and the rest."

"I'm impressed," Matthew said, nodding.

"It gets the job done," James said, unable to keep another smile from appearing.

"I go to the gym at least twice a week, and that's where we're going." Matthew made a right turn.

"Really?" James asked as his hands dropped to his sides, and he sat up straighter in the seat.

"Yep."

"Oh, I can't," he said as his shoulders slumped a little. "I don't have any workout clothes with me."

"Oh, that's not a problem. There's a sports shop next door to the gym. Therefore, we can stop there first."

"But I can't afford to buy new clothes right now." James shook his head.

"You worry a lot about money, don't you, James?" Matthew asked, pulling off the road and into a parking lot.

"I worry a little about it, but not a lot. I just prefer to spend my money selectively."

"Well, I try to do the same thing, too," Matthew said, parking the car.

"That reminds me, I have the change for you from the taxi ride."

"Great. You can use it towards your workout gear," Matthew said, opening the car trunk. As he opened the door, he added, "Come, we are here."

"Aren't you going to put the hood up?"

"Nah, I leave it open sometimes. It'll be okay."

He took a red and black gym bag out of the trunk, and James followed him.

A few hours later, they left the gym.

"Wait," James said, slowing his steps, "is that someone in your car?"

"Where?" Matthew asked, looking up

from his gym bag. "Yes, it is my car. Who's that in it?"

Matthew quickened his steps.

When they reached the car, they saw a man who looked to be in his fifties, but he could be younger, sitting in the driver's seat with his hands on the steering wheel. He was dressed in rags, and a low, continuous humming sound came from his throat.

In a steady, firm tone, Matthew said, "Excuse me? What are you doing in my car?"

The man looked up, and like a child caught with a mouthful of forbidden food, he froze, but after a few seconds, he stood on the seat, jumped out of the car, and ran away. James and Matthew looked at each other, and James gave him the "I told you so" look.

"There's always the first time for something," Matthew said, "and maybe now I'll think twice before leaving the top off."

"Oh yeah," James said, watching Matthew as he examined the inside of the car.

A short time later, James stepped out of the Ferrari at a bus stop. From there, he would catch a bus to take him home. A line of people was at the bus stop, and he was thankful he had walked with his backpack. He was grateful for his knapsack because there were no empty seats when the bus pulled up about five minutes later, and he stepped onto the bus. The new things Matthew bought for him were on his back, and he did not need to struggle with standing and holding bags.

Matthew wanted to take him home, but James wouldn't allow him to do so. He didn't want to cause his mom any more pain. As he stood on the bus, the memory of shopping and then working out at the gym with Matthew brought a huge smile to his face. The smile almost turned into a laugh but was drowned by waters of guilt that flooded his heart.

How can I do this to my mom? How can I enjoy spending time with the man who turned her life upside down and has gotten away with it? Oh Lord, this can't be right. It can't be. He sighed.

I need to talk to my uncle and aunt. Since he had to pass their home on the bus to his home, he decided to visit them.

"How can I have a relationship with him when he doesn't even believe he did anything wrong?" James asked, sitting on the edge of the chair in his uncle's and aunt's living room.

They nodded, sitting in the chair opposite him. His Aunt Amanda had prepared for him a large cup of hot cocoa and four slices of toast with cheese. They had just finished dinner when they heard a knocking on the front door.

"I can't do this to my mom," he said, shaking his head.

"Do you want to have a relationship with your father, James?" Uncle Thomas asked.

"I had a great time with him today, and dinner last Saturday was not completely bad."

"And what about his parents?" his aunt asked.

"The jury is still out on them, but Tracy seems nice."

They nodded.

"I want to have a relationship with him, but if I do, I will betray Mom, and I don't want to do that to her."

"Then talk with her, tell her what you are thinking and take it from there. She loves you, son, and she just wants what's best for you," his uncle said.

"Okay, okay," James replied, nodding before sighing.

He braced back in the floral upholstery chair as thoughts raced through his mind, and something pulled at his memory. He shifted his head to the right and pulled out the memory.

"Uncle Thomas," he said, looking at him, "do you know where my grandmother, your mommy, is working right now?"

Thomas' mouth fell open, but he closed it and thought briefly before answering, "No, I don't. I wasn't expexting that question. Why did you ask?"

"It's just something that Tracy said, but that's not the main reason why I'm asking. I'm asking because you and Mom never talk about her or Granddad, and I've never met them. All I know about them is that she works in security, and Granddad was a mason. Please tell me what happened between you guys."

"I would like to, but you should talk to your Mom about them first. You and Sammy have been outstanding at not asking us about them; we are thankful for that. So, thank you."

James shrugged. "That's okay, uncle. Sammy and I had questions, but we realized that my mom's past upsets her, so we tried to avoid asking questions about it. Now, knowing better, I'm glad we did ask."

"I understand," his uncle said, nodding.

"Also, Aunty Amanda's parents were and are still so good to me that I didn't and still don't lack the attention of grandparents. Still, it would have been good to have them in Sammy and my lives."

His uncle nodded.

"It's always been Sammy and me. Even after Mom and I moved out, it was still the two of us until Stacy came along.

"Yes," his aunt said, "and that day when the Sunday School teacher presented the gospel and then the invitation to be saved, both of you repented."

"Yes," James said, nodding and smiling. "From time to time, both of you would tell me about the Lord Jesus and how He came into this world, died for my sins, was buried and then rose from the grave on the third day."

"Yes," Uncle Thomas said.

"Still, I did not repent. However, for some reason, on that day in Sunday School, I was so convicted of my sins that I had to get right with God."

"Praise the Lord," Uncle Thomas said.

"Yes," James said, "but now Sammy's away, and when he gets back, I don't know how he'll take not being here when I found out about ...all of this."

"Yeah, he would have wanted to be here for you, but don't worry, all of us are here for each other," his aunt said, moving forward in the chair.

"Yes," James said, exhaling heavily. He rubbed his forehead.

"The Lord is in control, son, and He loves you very much. We love you very much, too."

James nodded, and unexpectedly, tears gathered in his eyes. As he tried to blink them away, a sound escaped from his throat, and tears overtook him.

His aunt rushed over to him.

"It's okay, son, it's okay. Let it all out, let it all out," she said, rubbing his back.

After a while, James wiped the tears from his face with the tissue his aunt brought with the cup of hot cocoa and toast with cheese he had earlier.

"I'm okay. I'll be okay," James said, "but what about Mom? I have her and the three of you guys, but I also have the Lord, and she doesn't have Him. She's been carrying this for so long, but only He can truly help her. I've been sharing Him with her since being saved three years ago, and you guys have been doing so forever, but she has not responded yet."

"Well, we will keep living the Christian life, sharing Jesus with her, keep praying, and I know that the Holy Spirit will keep working on her heart," Uncle Thomas said.

"Yes," James replied. Silence fell between them for a few seconds. Then James said, "I'm also worried about her health. She is eating as usual but still losing weight, and sometimes, she doesn't seem all right. I don't know. Maybe it's just stress, but everything doesn't seem right."

"Really?" Aunty Amanda asked.

"Yes," James replied, "maybe it's nothing, but I'll try to get her to go to the doctor."

His uncle and aunt exchanged a look of concern that James missed because he looked down at the watch on his left hand.

"I better get going," James said, yawning, "thanks for dinner and being here for my mom and me."

CHAPTER 16
YOU DID WHAT?

The following day, Janice sat at the dining room table with numerous papers in front of her.

As usual, she had enough time to meet her client's deadline but wanted to finish the job a few days before. However, no matter how hard she tried, she could not concentrate on her work. Her thoughts drifted to the security safe at the bottom of her wardrobe. Once again, Matthew Ward was forcing his way into her life, and again, she felt powerless to stop him.

Oh yes, I can, she thought.

She dropped the blue folder, and the breeze it created caused a few of the papers on the table to jump out of position. She stood and freed herself from between the chair and the table. She then hurried to her bedroom, and a few minutes later, she was sitting on the bed with the safe open. She held a silver gun in her hands and gently caressed it.

"Why do I still have you?" she asked

quietly, then whispered, "Why haven't I gotten rid of you?"

Thomas did not know she had the gun because she never told him. When she told him about the attack, she left out the part about it falling out of his pocket. So, she hid it from them when she went to live with him and Amanda. There were no loose boards in their home. Tiles were throughout the house. Neither could she find a safe place anywhere in the house. So, she kept it wrapped in a cloth and buried it in a hole she dug under the front stairs. Then, when she and James moved into their own rental house, she unearthed it the day before moving and took it with them. Afterwards, she bought a small, grey, security-safe box that was small enough to fit in the back of her wardrobe.

It was illegal to own a gun without a permit, but she could still buy the bullets for it. The box with its twelve bullets was still sitting in the safe, and she glanced at them.

"Why do I still have you?" She turned over the gun and asked, "Are you here for me, Matthew Ward, or both of us?"

Janice became lost in her thoughts, but she was slowly drawn back to the present by the telephone's ringing. Only one phone was in the house, and it was in the living room. She sighed loudly.

"Who could it be?" she wondered as she

debated whether to answer it or allow the answering machine to pick it up. She decided to get it because something about how it was ringing bothered her. She quickly replaced the gun in the security safe, closed it and returned it to the back of her wardrobe. She speed-walked to the living room.

"Hello?" she greeted, trying to control her breathing.

There was no response from the other end.

"Hello?" she asked again.

There was still no response.

"Is someone there?"

Janice took the phone from her ear and looked at it. She wondered if the person had hung up before she'd gotten to it. She shrugged and was about to put down the receiver.

"Hello Janice," a horsed voice said, and it paused before adding, "This is your mother. How are you?"

The phone slipped from her hand, but she caught it before it hit the floor. She dropped into the closest chair.

"Hi," Janice said, "I'm doing well. How are you?"

"Oh, so, so. I've been fighting a cold for a few days, but I'll live."

"The flu is spreading these days."

"Yes," her mother said.

Silence followed.

"Listen, Janice," she said after a few seconds, "I need to see you. Can you pass by my house tomorrow or sometime soon?"

"What is it?" Janice asked, her brow arching.

"I haven't seen or talked to you for almost twenty years. Will you come?"

The gentleness in her mother's voice took her by surprise. It took her back to the night of her attack and how gentle she was with her. It tugged at her heart.

"Yes, sure, I'll come," she said, "I can come by tomorrow. What time is good for you?"

"Anytime is good for me. I'll be at home the entire day."

"What about around eleven, just before lunch?"

"That's fine," she said before a coughing spell overtook her.

"Are you okay?"

"I'm fine, I'm fine. I'll see you tomorrow. Bye."

"Okay, bye," Janice said.

Janice stared at the phone for a few seconds before putting it down.

What was that? she wondered as her mind drifted to the last time she saw her mother. *What does she want after all this time? How did she get my number?*

She sighed.

"Well, I'll find out soon enough."

Janice sat silently for a few minutes, thinking about nothing in particular. She got up and went back to work at the dining room table. She buried herself in her career, and later that day, when James returned home, as with everything to do with her mother, she did not mention the phone call to him.

The following day, at a few minutes to eleven o'clock, Janice walked on an unfamiliar but familiar street. It was the street she had driven away on so many years ago.

The rain was pounding the land for most of the day, but as Janice walked down the road, it was reduced to a drizzle and stopped. She closed the purple umbrella she was sheltering under and shook off some of the water on it. The umbrella was small enough to fit in her handbag, but she always ensured it was dry before putting it in her bag. So, she held it unclasped in her hand.

Janice saw no one else on the street, but when she glanced at the windows of some of the houses, she saw a few faces peeping out from behind curtains. She smiled to herself and wondered if any of them recognized her.

She drew closer to her mother's home, and when she saw it, to her surprise, dark green paint replaced the faded blueish-green paint she had left. Several new boards also replaced the rotting ones. The place looked better than Janice had ever seen, and her mouth involuntary fell open, and she almost tripped over her feet. She steadied herself, turned into the unfenced yard, and walked up the replaced wooden steps. She lifted her hand to knock on the door, but to her surprise, it swung open, and her mother stood there.

Janice stared at her mother as they both studied each other's faces. Janice saw the aging that she had expected, but not in the way that she was hoping. Her mother was ageing well, and this sent a slight stabbing pain into her chest. She was disappointed to see her mom looking as well as she did. She had envisioned her mother ageing terribly with wrinkles all over her body. Yes, there were wrinkles, but they were all in the right places, and the numerous grey hairs on her head only helped to enhance and soften her features. She wore a sleeveless blue and white cotton dress with buttons running down the front. She was a picture of tenderness that her eyes still did not hold.

Nevertheless, something was different in them. Something that Janice could not quite put her hands on.

What was it? Maybe it's happiness or sadness. No, that can't be.

"Hi Janice, come in, come in," her mother greeted as she stepped aside to allow her to enter the house.

"Thanks," Janice murmured, entering.

She had also envisioned the house's inside to be a time capsule, but to her amazement, it was not. Gold-coloured curtains were hanging at the windows. New flowered chairs sat in the living room. Cream and white paint graced the walls, and several photos, a clock and other hangings lined them. Janice had never seen these things in the house before. There was also an enlarged photo of her mother, Thomas and her when they were younger. She was sitting on her mother's lap, and Thomas stood close to them. Her mother had the original photo in an album, and this was Janice's favourite photo of them.

"Sit, sit," she was encouraged after slipping off her heel-less black shoes and following her into the living room.

"How are you?" her mother asked, smiling at her.

Who is this person? Janice wondered.

"I'm good," she replied, "What about you? How is the cold?"

"Still here, but a bit better than yesterday."

They talked about the flu for a few minutes before they lapped into silence.

"Mom, why am I here?" Janice asked.

"You were never one to beat around the bush, were you, Janice?" she asked, laughing softly.

"That's just me," she replied, lifting and dropping her shoulders.

"How is my grandson?"

Did she just say, Grandson? How does she know that I have a son?

"He's doing fine, really fine," she replied, nodding.

"Do you have a photo of him with you?"

"A... a photo?" Janice asked with a frown. *Who is this woman?*

"Yes, can I see a photo of him?"

Janice stared at her. *Is this the same person who wanted me to kill my son? Now she wants to see a photo of him? What's going on here?*

"What's going on here, Mom? Did you ask me over here to talk about my son?"

"Let me look at you."

She looked at Janice from her corn-rowed head to the pink linen shirt tucked into her blue jeans and black shoes at the door.

"The years have been good to you, child, but you look a little tired, and you look as though you've recently lost a few pounds," she said.

"Well, yeah, work has been keeping me busy, and I can do without those pounds," Janice snapped and folded her arms over her chest.

"Oh, where are my manners? Would you like something to eat?" her mother asked, rising from the chair.

Janice opened her mouth to object as she dropped her hands from her chest, but her mother walked past her and headed for the kitchen. Janice's shoulders tensed, but she slowly and loudly inhaled and quickly let it out, but it did not help her. She heard her mother moving around in the kitchen she and thought about getting up and leaving.

Stay calm, stay calm.

She took in a few more deep breaths, and this time, as she slowly let them out, her shoulders relaxed, and she slumped her shoulders and slowly braced back in the chair.

"I baked this fruit cake yesterday," her mother called out from the kitchen.

Before or after you decided to call me? Janice wanted to ask, but she held her tongue.

She knows I like the way she makes fruit cake, Janice thought. *It's never too moist or dry and always full of red, yellow and black cherries and raisins.*

Her mother returned to the living room with a medium-sized saucer and a large triangular piece of colourful fruit cake resting on it. She also carried a tall glass of purple-coloured drink, a cup holder and a light purple tissue.

"Here you go," she said, giving her the plate. She then placed the cup holder on the glass top, square black table before placing the glass on it.

"Thank you," Janice said, taking it from her hand.

"You're welcome."

Janice ate the delicious cake in silence, and occasionally, she picked up the glass from the table and drank the grape drink in it.

"This cake tastes delicious," Janice said, with her mouth still full.

"I remember how much you liked it, but I wasn't sure if you still do."

Janice nodded as she drank the grape drink.

"I will wrap up a piece for you to take home. How about your son? Would he like a piece to eat, too?"

"As long as it's edible, he'll eat it," Janice said as a sudden laugh escaped her.

"I guess he takes after you with that. I never had to worry about what to cook for you because you always ate whatever I placed in front of you."

"Well," she replied, "you are a good cook."

Janice emptied her plate and glass and wiped her mouth with the tissue.

"Do you want another piece?"

"No. No, thanks, that was just right," Janice said.

"Are you sure?

"Mom, when you called me yesterday, you said you wanted to talk with me about something. What is it? Why am I here, Mom?"

"Yes," she sighed heavily. "But let me take this to the kitchen first."

She got up, took the dishes from Janice's hand, and went to the kitchen. When she returned, Janice leaned back in the chair with her arms folded. Her mother sat down, and after clearing her throat, she said, "About six weeks ago, I went to work to guard a real estate company."

"Okay," Janice said.

"They wanted a security guard because they had problems with one client. Among other things, the client had threatened to vandalize their property." She coughed, and mucus rattled in her throat. "I came across an old acquaintance there. He was the driver for one of the real estate owners. So we were catching up, and he told me something I think you have the right to know."

Janice's hands slowly dropped into her lap.

"What thing?" she questioned.

"He asked me how you were and said he was sorry for the terrible thing that happened to you."   She coughed again. "He would not tell me who he heard it from but said that he heard someone paid "big money" for a male prostitute to visit you because of what I did."

A kaleidoscope of emotions played across her mother's face as Janice watched her.

"What?" Janice quietly asked as she moved forward in the chair.

Involuntarily and instantly, the living room began to spin, and it lasted for several seconds. Janice grabbed her thighs to steady herself. Her mother hesitated for a few seconds before continuing.

"There was a mix-up with my work schedule on the night of your attack."

"Yes," Janice said, "Somehow, I still remember that."

"At least that's what I thought. I thought it was a mix-up, but it wasn't. It was purpose work to get me out of the house for when the guy would turn up here."
Janice wanted to stand, but she was still feeling dizzy, which kept her in her seat. She braced back in the chair.

I need to see a doctor, she thought. *It's been over fifteen, sixteen years since I've dealt with this, but I wonder if my thyroid problems are returning.*

"Why would one of your acquaintances do this to me?" she managed to ask.

Her mother cleared her throat and shifted uncomfortably in the chair before answering. "A month or so before your attack, a former co-worker's cousin tried to break into a store my partner and I were guarding. We caught him. Then we thought it would send a message to other thieves not to mess with our security company if we give him a good beating."

"How badly did you guys beat him?"

Her mother was silent for a long moment, and Janice quietly waited as she willed her dizziness to go away. Her mother exhaled tremblingly, saying, "My partner and I went overboard because after we beat him with our batons, we put it into places it should not go."

"You did what?" Janice exclaimed after instantly understanding what her mother meant.

Janice jumped out of the chair but immediately fell back into it.

"Are you okay?" her mother immediately asked, frowning.

"I'm fine, fine," Janice said, steadying herself in the chair. "Why would you do that to him or anyone for that fact?"

"That was not all," she said, still frowning as she rubbed her forehead. "We also took photos of what we did and secretly passed it around in certain places."

Janice stared at her.

"We didn't know he was our co-worker's cousin, and the co-worker never said anything about it. We even showed him the photos. Although, looking back now, I can see that there was something there."

"And that would have made it alright?" Janice asked in dismay.

"I'm not saying that."

"Then what are you saying?"

"Do you want me to continue or not?" her mother asked, her voice rising slightly.

Janice stared at her, and her mother stared back at her.

"Go ahead," Janice finally said, lowering her eyes.

"Alright," her mother said, and after pausing some more, she continued. "This co-worker messed with the work schedule to get me away from home that night. Somehow, my ex-co-worker made a copy of the house key and gave it to your attacker so that he could get into the house."

"Wait a minute," Janice said, "he used a key to get into the house, and he didn't get in through your bedroom window?"

"Hmm, the bedroom window, you remembered it."

"Of course. You thought I'd left it opened."

"Yes, and you thought I did, but your

attacker did it. It was to throw me off."

"But it didn't throw you off. Honestly, it didn't even have any impact on you. You thought it was Roger or someone I knew."

"Yes, yes," her mother said, nodding, "and I am sorry about that."

Janice stared at her mother as her mind fought to process what she had just heard.

Finally, finally, she thought. *I've found the answer to my "why me" question.* Suddenly, Janice felt exhausted, and her shoulders dropped. A cry escaped her lips, and her upper body shook as tears poured down her cheeks like a running faucet. Her mother sprang to her feet and placed an arm around her shoulders, but Janice shook it off. She drew her legs up into the chair and rocked her body from side to side as mournful cries poured out of her. Her mother threw her hands helplessly into the air before returning to her seat, and as she watched Janice weeping, tears quietly ran out of her eyes, and she wiped them away with the palms of her hands.

As Janice cried, mournful sounds, but no words, continued to escape through her throat and lips. She mourned for a long time.

When the tears stopped, she slowly wiped away the wetness on her cheeks before slowly lifting her head to look at her mother.

"I'm so sorry, Janice."

Janice looked at her for a few seconds before she nodded once. She lowered her feet and slowly rose from the chair. Her dizziness was gone.

"Can I use your washroom?" she asked.

"Of course. You know where it is," was the instant reply.

"Thanks," she mumbled and headed for it.

When she entered the washroom, Janice staggered slightly because of its changes. Instead of the familiar wood, cream tiles graced the floor and unfamiliar blue toilet mats laid on the tiles. A white sink replaced the peach one, and this was the first time she'd seen the blue and white shower curtains hanging in front of the shower area. She quietly pulled aside the curtains and peeped inside the shower area. Grey tiles, instead of the familiar grey concrete, greeted her. A new shower-head and piping system were also there.

"Hmm," escaped her throat before she quietly pulled back the curtains.

She stood and surveyed the washroom and saw that the miniature painting of a little girl kneeling in prayer was still on the wall. She nodded, then tidied up. She returned to the living room, where she found her mother standing with a peach paper bag in her hand.

"The cake is in here," she said, stretching it out.

"Thanks," Janice said, taking it from her.

She walked over to the chair where her black handbag was bracing. She picked up the bag and opened it, placed the cake inside it, and zipped the bag shut.

"I have to go," she said, walking to the front door.

"Yeah, I know."

Janice pushed her feet into her shoes.

"Here, drink. It will help your throat," Janice's mom said.

She looked up to find her mother holding out a glass to her.

"It's water with a little lemon in it."

"Thanks," Janice said, slowly taking it from her.

She drank all of it and only then realized how much her throat was parched.

"I know that I haven't been the best mother in the world to you and your brother, but I have changed, and I don't think it is too late for me to ask you and him to give me another chance."

The glass in Janice's hand almost slipped out of it.

"Thanks, thanks for the water," she said, stretching the glass to her.

She took it.

"I've been seeing someone for the past two years, and he's perfect for me... we are perfect for each other," her mother said, smiling slightly.

"I have to go now," Janice said, pointing to the door over her shoulder, "I cannot deal with anything else right now."

"Yes, I understand, but will you at least think about what I've said and have a talk with your brother for me, too?"

Janice nodded yes before turning to face the door. She briefly bent to pick up the umbrella she had placed beside her shoes. The umbrella was still wet; if she were home, she would have dried it off and stored it away. Yes, she could have asked her mother for some tissues to dry it off, but with the possibility of it raining on her way home, there was no point in drying it off prematurely. Janice opened the door.

"I'll talk with you soon," her mother called behind her.

"Bye," Janice said and quickly walked out of the house.

The rain was still holding off, and Janice hoped it would remain that way until James and she returned home.

As Janice made her way home, a great weight felt lifted from her shoulders, but at the same time, the sadness looming over her for the past twenty years drew closer and tried, as she did, she could not push it away.

Janice made it through the front door,

and just as she closed it behind her, the rain began to drum its rhythm on the rooftop. She smiled.

"Ah," she exclaimed as she removed her shoes, "I beat you, but James may have to deal with you."

She tried to keep the smile on her face as she made her way to the bedroom, but exhaustion suddenly overtook her, and the smile immediately disappeared, and her shoulders slumped. She entered the room, and after leaving the door partly open, she crawled into the bed, and as soon as her body rested on it, she was fast asleep.

Janice slept, and when she awoke, she felt as though she had just woken up from a long, long rest. She took a shower, and to her surprise, she hummed while showering. She could not remember the last time she'd hummed.

After showering, she dressed in red shorts and a white T-shirt with square boxes on it. The rain had stopped, and she hoped James would get in before it started up again.

She went to the living room, and after sitting down, she took up the telephone and sped-dialled her brother's home number.

"Hello?" Thomas answered after three rings.

"Hi, Teddy Bear."

"Hi Jan, how are you?"

"I'm good. Hmm, I saw Mom today. She called me yesterday, and I went by to see her today."

"What? Wow," Thomas said, "I didn't see that coming. Is she okay? What did she say?"

"She has a cold, but apart from that, she's okay."

"Good. What did Mom want?"

"I don't want to talk about it over the phone, but she filled in the gaps about my attack."

The phone line went silent for a few seconds before Thomas asked, "What do you mean?"

"I'll tell you about it tomorrow. I don't want to do it on the phone."

"I have time today. We can come by right now if you want," Thomas said expectantly.

Janice chuckled. "No, no. I want to talk to James first. He'll be in soon. He had another job interview today."

"I'll drop by tomorrow, and we'll talk then."

"Okay, alright," Thomas said, slowly drawing out the words.

"Thomas."

"Yeah?"

"Thanks for being a great big brother and returning for me."

"Well, thanks for being a wonderful sister, and I'm glad I came back, too."

"I also want to say that I'm going to talk with James about Mom tonight, too."

"Okay," was the instant reply, "and when Sammy returns, I'll do the same."

"Okay," she replied, nodding.

She smiled, and the line was quiet for a few seconds before Thomas said, "Wait, hold on a minute. Amanda is saying something."

He was gone for a few seconds.

"Amanda wants to talk to you, so I'll put her on, and we'll see you tomorrow, the Lord willing."

"Do I have to?" Janice asked, trembling her voice.

"Yes, you do," came the excited reply.

"Alright. Let me guess, um, you got a new client for me?"

"How did you know?" Amanda exclaimed. "Did Thomas tell you?"

"Nope, I can tell from your voice."

"This one is not like the last one," Amanda immediately replied.

"No?" Janice asked.

"No. It is one of our clients. One of his staff left him unexpectedly, and right now, they have more work than they can handle, so I told him about you."

Janice waited for her to continue as memories of the most recent client Amanda referred to her floated to the surface of her mind. She was not going to forget this client anytime soon. After Janice completed the client's income tax paperwork, she was not happy with the amount of money she was getting back. She insisted that she should be getting back more money. So, she demanded the return of her documents along with her deposit. Janice returned them without arguing. Then, about three weeks later, the client returned, apologized for her behaviour and asked her to take her back as a client. She explained that three of the tax servicing businesses she went to were charging twice as much as Janice did and calculating even less than Janice had calculated for her return.

"He wants you to call him tomorrow," Amanda told her. "Do you have a pen and paper?"

"Yes, go ahead," Janice said, picking up the pen and paper on the stand beside the phone.

Amanda told her, and she wrote down the information.

"Thanks, Amanda, you're always looking out for me."

"Always," Amanda said with a smile in her voice.

"I have to go now, but make sure that Thomas fills you in on what I said."

"I will," Amanda said.

"Okay. Bye."

"Bye."

As she put down the receiver, the rain started to dance on the rooftop slowly, and once again, she hoped James would not get caught in it on his way home.

Janice slumped in the chair and thought about the visit to her mother's home. She silently replayed what her mother told her about the attack, and every time she replayed her mother's words, pain like knitting needles stabbed at her heart. However, she fought the tears that surged because of the pain and kept them away.

Janice was taking a deep breath when she heard running feet. The footsteps stopped at the door, and she listened to the sound of keys jingling. The door unlocked and pushed open. James entered the house.

"Mom, Mom!" he called out, turning to lock the door.

"I'm right here," she sang out.

"Oh," he said after turning his head toward her voice.

The rain had drenched his light brown, long-sleeved formal shirt and long black pants. Water ran down his face from his recently cut, short, and curly high-top hair.

"The rain caught you, I see," she said.

He locked the door before looking down at his clothes.

"Yeah, but I was so close to home before

it started to pour down."

"You have to get out of those clothes before you catch a cold."

"Yeah."

"How was the job hunt today?" she asked.

"It went well. I start on Monday at Levi's Magazine House, and the Wards do not own it," he replied, bending to take off his shoes and socks.

"Congrats, son. I knew it wouldn't take you too long to find another job."

"Yeah, thank the Lord because, for a moment there, I was starting to get worried.".

"Well, I wasn't, and I want to hear all about it, but first, go, take a shower and come and sit here with me. I need to talk to you."

James looked over at her and studied her face for a few seconds. She smiled briefly at him. He wanted to hear what she had to say right away. He thought of quickly changing out of his wet clothes and rushing back to her. However, his mom was right. It was best to get the rainwater out of his hair and off his body with a shower.

"Okay," he said, lifting his hand into the air, "I'll take a quick shower."

"You don't have to rush because I'm not going anywhere."

Nevertheless, James did rush and was thankful for the shower because after being out of the home for the entire day, he just needed a shower. So he hurriedly dressed in the long green jeans and white untucked shirt he wore yesterday. He was hungry, too, but that could wait.

"Okay, here I am," he said, quickly covering the distance between them and sitting beside her.

Janice studied his face briefly before saying, "I went to see my mom today."

"What? You did?" James asked, his eyes enlarging.

"Yes, she called me yesterday, and I went to her place today."

"Really? Wow! How is she? Is she still living where you grew up?"

"She is recovering from the flu, and yes, she is still living where your uncle and I grew up."

"Wow, that's something," James said. "Mom, do you know that this is the most you've ever told me about my grandmother?"

"Yes," she replied, nodding. "I know that you had questions, but I knew that if I spoke to you about her or your granddad, your birth would come up, and I was not ready for that."

"I understand. So does this mean you are now ready to talk about them? Can I now ask you questions about them?"

The rain suddenly increased its beating on the house, and Janice glanced over at the window.

"It's certainly coming down now," James said, glancing over at a window before looking back at his mother.

"Yes, it is, and yes, we can talk about your grandparents," Janice said. "But not right now. Right now, I want to tell you about the conversation, if I can call it that, that I had with your grandmother today."

"Okay," James said quickly.

"I think I told you once that my mother worked as a security guard, right?"

"Yes, you did."

"Good. Recently, your grandmother was stationed at a real estate company. There, she ran into someone she knew, and through this person, she found out why Matthew Ward assaulted me."

James' mouth dropped open, but he quickly closed it and then asked, "What? What do you mean?"

"Yes," she said, nodding.

"What, how could that be? I thought you did not report it to the police. I thought you did not tell anyone about it?"

"You're correct, but don't forget that Matthew Ward and his friends know about it, too."

"Oh, yes. I don't know what I was thinking," James said, lightly tapping his forehead.

"It's okay," Janice said, lightly touching

him on the knee.

He nodded.

"She learned that it happened because of something she and a co-worker did to another co-worker's cousin. It was payback for them."

"What?" James exclaimed, "Payback?"

"They hired Matthew Ward to come to my house that night, but I don't know how involved he was in this "payback." I just know for certain that they hired him to do what he did to me."

"Oh, Mom, I am so sorry."

"If only I'd just locked my bedroom door..."

"No, Mom, no, please don't go there. None of this is your fault. None of it."

She smiled absentmindedly at him.

"Mom, you have to press charges against him," James suddenly exclaimed.

"What?" she asked, struggling to pull away from her thoughts. "What did you say?"

"I said that you have to press charges against my father. I don't know what the law says about how long someone has to report sexual assault cases, but you should talk to a lawyer and file charges against him."

Janice was silently thoughtful.

"You can't keep punishing yourself for other people's crimes. You can't keep going on like this. It has to end, Mom."

"But if I go to a lawyer and all of this comes out, it will put you in the spotlight, and I can't do this to you."

"You haven't done anything wrong, and neither have I," James said, frowning. "So what if we are in the spotlight?"

"I mean, he is your father."

"Yes, and you are my mother."

Janice studied his face for a few seconds.

"No," she said, shaking her head. "I can't do this to you."

James reached out, lightly squeezed her face between his palms, and then let them go.

"You haven't said anything to me about it yet, but I know you would like to have a relationship with your father, and if I go to the police, it will only get in the way of you doing so."

"Mom, you are always thinking about what's best for me because you love me, but I love you too, and I'm thinking about what's best for you, too."

"But–"

"Have you talked with Uncle and Aunty about what Grandma said?"

"No, not as yet. I wanted to talk with you about it first."

James nodded as he said, "Well, that is my advice. I suggest you talk with a lawyer about it and, if you still can, press charges against him. Then, when you find out who else was involved in the attack, press charges against them, too!"

Janice reached out and hugged him tightly.

"My son, my son, my son," she whispered. "My beautiful boy."

She let go of him after a few minutes.

"Oh, son," she said, "I thought I made peace with this years ago, but now I don't know."

"I understand, Mom, but the Lord Jesus is the only One who can give you true peace."

Janice nodded.

"Yes, I know," she said, "but I have been carrying this for so long. I don't know how to stop carrying it. I don't know who I would be without it."

"Then give it to Jesus. He can take care of it and you."

"Oh, son," she said, shaking her head.

"The Lord Jesus loves you, Mom. He loves you so much that He died for your sins. He paid the price to set you free."

Janice took a deep breath and slowly let it out. Then she was silent for a little while, and James held his breath, waiting for her to speak.

"Will you pray with me, son?" she finally said.

"Yes, I will," he instantly replied.

"Thank you," she said, closing her eyes
and slightly bowing her head.
"Oh Lord Jesus..." she began.

ABOUT THE AUTHOR

A. M. Linton is a wife and mother of two. She is also the author of Torn Between Love, Religion and Responsibility, A Little on Puberty for Boys and A Little on Symptoms Associated with Menopause. A few of her short stories were also published in The Barbados Advocate Newspaper.

MORE BOOKS
BY A. M. LINTON

Torn Between Love, Religion,
and Responsibility

A Little on Puberty for Boys

A Little on Symptoms
Associated with Menopause